Promise in the Void

Promise in the Void

Eileen MacDonald

Enjoy my grandmother's book! Rebekah Allen

PROMISE IN THE VOID

Author: Eileen MacDonald (1912-1998)

Publication Project Manager: Rebekah Allen, Airdrie, Alberta

Editor: Jennifer Kaddoura, Victoria, British Columbia

Front cover photograph by Sam Allen

Back cover photo of Canadian soldiers in Normandy by Conseil Régional de Basse-Normandie Archives Nationales du CANADA (Public domain) via Wikimedia Commons

Published by Rebekah Allen, Airdrie, Alberta

ISBN978-1-77354-026-9

Publication assistance and digital printing in Canada by

PageMasterPublishing.ca

About Eileen

The publication of this novel is dedicated to the memory of Eileen Mary MacDonald, the author of *Promise in the Void*. A gifted lady and loyal Canadian, Eileen sought to work out many of her life experiences through poetry and creative storytelling.

Eileen was born in Ahmednagar, India, in 1912 to Irish parents stationed there under the British military. She grew up in Ireland with three siblings and faced economic and social struggles. Approaching adulthood, she was determined to immigrate to Canada to find hope and opportunity.

In 1930, at the tender age of 18 years old, she and a girlfriend journeyed from Ireland to Canada by ship. They travelled from Quebec to Alberta by train and arrived at the YWCA in Edmonton. Being industrious, Eileen put an ad in the paper (with the YWCA's phone number) stating, "Two Irish lasses willing to work for room and board." From this ad, Eileen connected with a local Irish family, the Rutleys, and thus began her Canadian friendships. She obtained employment at the Great Western Garment Company in Edmonton and became known for her 'quickness' as a seamstress.

In 1933, she ventured into the Peace River Country of Alberta, where she married and gave birth to her four children. Eileen faced significant adversity, but she found great solace in reading and writing. She was interested in current events and the way people solved problems in their lives.

In the mid-1940s, at about the time her first marriage began to crumble, Eileen began to write her full-length novel about a war bride who, like herself, immigrated to Canada to follow her dreams for a better life. With limited resources and many life challenges, Eileen continued to work on the manuscript while raising a family, remarrying and becoming one of Canada's first female customs officers. Eileen wrote this story over several decades. While it is a work of fiction, many aspects of the story paralleled her life and were personally meaningful.

In 1997, with failing health, she gave all copies of the manuscript to her granddaughter, Rebekah Allen. Eileen requested that the manuscript be published, but if that was not possible, Rebekah was to leave the manuscript in a suitcase for her own grandchildren to find someday. In bestowing the manuscript upon Rebekah, Eileen bequeathed more than she could ever know in memory, inspiration, and love.

Eileen Mary MacDonald (née McCready) at age 17

Promise in the Void

Chapter One

*H*elen squeezed back into the corner of the worn old couch. She was unaware of the over-plump cousin who crowded her. Unaware, too, of the sea of faces peering through the flickering firelight in the familiar old parlour where she had spent many happy hours in bygone years.

The firelight was kind to the shabby old room, hiding the broken plaster of the ceiling, the peeling paint on the walls, the zigzag tape holding the window panes together. It lent an air of charm and comfort to the room, stirring up a grateful glow in Helen's heart.

Someone switched on the single bulb and its light bathed the old-fashioned chandelier, revealing its many sparkling facets. Helen saw her father's face clearly as he took his place before the fireplace and turned to face his friends, who gathered with an air of expectancy about them. He stood silently for a few moments while a slow smile crossed his weathered face as he took in the scene before him. The firelight outlined the tall figure, casting a halo round his head as he leaned slightly on his toes.

"Friends and neighbours and those nearer to us," he began, as the smile grew wistful. "We gathered in this room some twenty-two years ago, in that celebrated year of 1923. Many of you were here then, and you remember the occasion. It was a proud and happy one for my wife and me as we saw our baby, our first child, go through the baptismal rites of the church.

"Twenty years later, almost in the self-same spot, I stood here as I gave her to the man who promised to love, honour, and cherish her forever. Many of you were here for that occasion too. Even then, the thought of this parting tugged at my heart as I saw the Canada badge flash on the shoulder of his uniform. But I knew young love, and far be it from me, even now, to stand in the way of the girl who has been my pride and comfort through those twenty years."

Occasionally the old man's gaze rested on his eldest daughter's face, his eyes brimming with adoration. Helen was a tall, slim girl with soft-brown eyes, shining copper-coloured hair, and a perfect, fresh, English complexion. She wore the minimum of makeup because it was so unnecessary.

Her father went on to describe the friendship he had enjoyed with the young Canadian soldier and to recount some of the tales the young man had told of his homeland. Helen's mind wandered as she listened. While her dad regaled his listeners with stories of the prairies and foothills, gigantic mountain ranges and inland lakes, she was in a quiet glen where a mountain stream sang gaily over a miniature waterfall, where buttercups and daisies patterned the green banks, and where hawthorn and wild plum perfumed the air. In her private world the silence could be felt, broken only by the sound of the meadowlark or thrush in the hedgerow. She climbed over a quaint stone stile in early morning, as the heavy mist rose up from the marshes and the sun struggled bravely to break through. She watched quiet sheep on a gently sloping hillside—protected in a little field, neat and tidy as a pocket handkerchief—as the boy-shepherd sat on a mossy rock, blowing into his handmade whistle.

In her mind she was now back in the city, listening to the early-morning sounds of the factory's shrill blast as she turned in her bed, hearing the clatter of many hurrying feet on the pavement. She heard the rain rattle on the slate roof as it came down in torrents, rolling down the windowpanes.

Helen came back to the present with a start to hear her father's voice quicken with emotion as he said, "So, not long ago, we again gathered in this room to bid farewell to our dear wife and mother."

"Killed," he went on, "as you all know, by the enemy these boys came over to help us conquer. Now I am to lose my daughter to one of those boys. She goes with my heartfelt blessing and, I know, your many good wishes for her future happiness. My years will not be many, and I would never be happy very far from the fenced-in grave in our churchyard. But after I'm gone, I hope Sue, here," his glance touched the upturned face of his youngest daughter, "will one day find her way across the ocean to a new land and a newer, happier life beside her sister."

A small sob—more a catching-breath—answered him, and Sue bent her head as every gaze turned towards her. Helen was glad the attention was drawn away from her, but her heart went out to the girl, and she rose and crossed the room. Holding out her arms, she drew Sue up into them. Then, half turning, Helen faced the group, and in a few touching words she tried to express the happy memories she would carry with her to her new home. She thanked them for their parting gifts, saying she knew they represented real sacrifices in this time of stringent rationing and promising to cherish the gifts in the years to come.

Gradually, the gathering broke up in the slow way that such gatherings do. Someone said they must hasten home, and one by one they began to climb the stairs to dress for the outdoors, descending as they left for home. Helen and her dad stood in the narrow hallway shaking hands, and she promised to write. Young Sue fluttered upstairs and down, giving a help-ing hand where needed.

It was late when the last guest had gone, and the three gathered again in the parlour before the fireplace. The fire was low, and the room was already beginning to chill. Shadows lurked where the dim light failed to reach. Helen stooped to pick up a handkerchief that had fallen and then been kicked under a chair. Recognizing the faint perfume, she knew it was Aunt Min's. It was damp and wadded into a tight ball. Helen remembered her sitting there—overflowing the chair, making it creak—with an agitated look on her rosy face as she worked the handkerchief in her hands. Aunt Min was the pal and confidant of her childhood days. Helen dropped the damp little ball into the pocket of her dress, pressing it with her hand.

Sue was saying, "Johnny is a hero, isn't he? Never turned over once, not once, with all that racket as they dressed to go. I was hoping he would sleep through it. If he had wakened, his cries would have meant a parade through his room and, most likely, a bad night for all of us."

"Oh dear! I scarcely had time to give a thought to my son," Helen exclaimed. "But he did behave well, bless his little heart." She again put her arms around Sue and drew her tight as she looked over her sister's head into the fond face of the tall old man. He stood with one elbow on the mantelpiece, his head resting on his hand. "That," he said softly, "will be almost worse than losing you—to lose our Johnny." They were all quiet again. The rain continued to rattle on the windowpanes as the shadows darkened the corners. The house was cold, and Helen shivered.

She stood on the railway platform in the damp chill of an early morning and watched the hustle and bustle of the post-war travellers. Uniforms were still predominant, but there was a relaxed expression on the faces rushing past. There was also a grumpiness about folks, nowadays, as they began to demand improved conditions.

Dad, who had waited long in the queue at the ticket window, now came toward her through the crowd. A sharp pang touched her heart as she noticed that the broad shoulders had a tired stoop to them, the face deeply lined, the lips too tensely tight. He straightened and smiled as he caught sight of her running toward him. She threw herself into his arms and a longing flooded through her that the years could be rolled back, that this need only be one of those sunny Saturday mornings when they had made their way as a glad foursome down to this busy little station and climbed into the chugging short train on their way to some crowded beach.

Tearing herself from her father's embrace, she unwound little Johnny's plump arms from around Sue's neck. Sue, who was long past speaking, found the effort to subdue her sobs a challenging job. Helen kissed them hastily again and, without another word, turned toward the train. Picking up the suitcases, her father followed and placed them in the rack above her head. Seeing that she was comfortably settled, he placed a long kiss on her trembling lips, then passed his hand over Johnny's bright curls before wordlessly leaving them.

So it is that when life's vital moments arrive, words are inadequate, thoughts mere confusion, memory poor comfort, and courage elusive.

The seaport was a drab, gray place. No longer did the buildings reach down to the water's edge. They had been swept away, and in their place were long, neat rows of piled bricks and heaps of rubble. The sun danced and sparkled on the water, for the sky had cleared, and a fresh salt breeze blew in from the sea. Tiny tugs moved around and about the bigger ships lying at the wharf, as deep-throated signals echoed across the water.

Helen did not see the wharf or the heaps of rubble around her. Her eyes sought the sandy beach, the green hills, and the neat fields of her happier memories. Yet she loved the cities with their gray pavement too, for there, she knew, throbbed the heart of the isle—this Britain, this England.

As the ship pulled away, the apathy that had enveloped Helen since her parting from Dad and Sue withdrew slightly; she was distracted by the noise and excitement on board. Johnny had been sleepy and well-behaved on the train journey, but now he was restless and inclined to be cross and fretful.

In one way, this was a very good thing for Helen because it kept her fully occupied, with less time to worry, as the big ship slid softly from the pier and made her way out to sea. Helen did not see the sun setting on the skyline as the shore faded from sight. She was engaged in quieting her own screaming little bundle, settling him for the night amongst the sounds of many more just as irate and tired as he. Gradually, quietness descended upon the long rows of cabins and babies' cries ceased, only to be repeated occasionally. Operation diaper was well on its way.

Helen lay in her bunk, but sleep was far from her eyes and the worry that had been nagging her for weeks suddenly hovered in the darkness and refused to be suppressed any longer.

"No letter. No letter. No letter," beat through her brain with the throb of the engines. "No letter. No letter," with the motion of the waves. Nausea took hold of her, gripping her stomach as fear swept through her. Fear, such as she had escaped even in the air-raid shelters of the city, now pressed in and down upon her through the darkness and threatened to overwhelm her.

Suddenly, a soft knock on the cabin door aroused her to utter a feeble "come in." A short, white figure following the beam of a torch bent over her in the darkness and asked, in the beloved accent, "'Ow are ye, Luv? Feeling a'right?"

Helen found it impossible to form a reply. She buried her face in the pillow and sobbed for the first time.

"'Ere, Luv. Swallow these, they'll 'elp ye sleep. I'll bring ye a glass o' water, Duck. They's a good many as is feeling bad tonight."

She gratefully swallowed the tablets and drank the water and soon joined Johnny in his slumbers. But while he slept with an angelic baby smile playing about his lips, Helen passed through a nightmare of horror. She was on the edge of a cliff, with the ground beneath her crumbling. As she was slipping, slipping, she called, "Bill! Bill! Bill!" And he answered—oh so vaguely, so far away—and his voice throbbed with the engines, "No letter. No letter. No letter."

The first high-pitched wail along the corridor wakened her, and one by one other voices joined it as hungry babies roused to demand attention. She rose and attended Johnny. Though her head felt thick and spasms of seasickness gripped her, she made her way to the dining room, where she was overawed by the variety of food on the menu. With a half-guilty conscience, she ordered a large breakfast for herself and the baby. Her guilt increased when she found herself unable to do more than drink a glass of fruit juice and a cup of tea. By noon she was unable to lift her head from the bunk and was past caring when someone removed Johnny—along with his noisy chatter—and carried him off somewhere to be cared for.

After several days, Helen was able to make her way to the deck, where she lay on a deckchair and watched the heaving, gray waves as they rolled past the ship. She longed for the sight of land with intensity such as only the sea-weary know. She realized they had crossed the sea lanes where submarines and mines had haunted ships not many months earlier. Eventually, she perked up and began to take an interest in her surroundings.

She found, to her glad surprise, that one of the girls who shared her cabin was also on her way to Edmonton, Alberta. Together they wondered and planned, discussing and exchanging such small knowledge as each had of the city that neither had seen but which was to be their future home. Other girls soon joined the group, and presently there was a little fraternity of mothers and babies headed for the western province. Together they made plans to land in a group and secure adjacent seats on the train for the long journey across the continent, and to continue their friendship after arrival.

One evening, they clustered along the rail of the big ship as it swung into the St. Lawrence. Helen held her breath and pressed Johnny close to her heart as she drank in the scene of majestic beauty. The long rays of the sun reached out over the water, turning it to golden fire. The tall range of mountains hung as a beautiful backdrop to the magnificent view. Its grandeur left her trembling. This, then, was her new home. This was Canada!

Chapter Two

On landing, the girls found help on every side—someone willing to care for the babies, someone to help them onto the train, others to serve the inevitable cup of tea or warm the baby bottles—kindness and sympathy in abundance. The Red Cross ladies were everywhere, as were members of the different church denominations and clubs, each to give advice or help where needed.

On the first night of the train journey, all the children were restless and fussy. There was an air of tense excitement pervading the atmosphere. Wires had to be sent off, others were coming in reply as the train rushed on through the countryside.

Helen too had sent a wire, but she waited in vain for some acknowledgement from Bill. Her uneasiness increased as Johnny needed more and more attention, for he grew more feverish and restless by the hour. When evening fell, he was a sick little boy, and Helen found herself and the baby isolated and alone. Johnny showed symptoms of measles.

"Just my luck!" she thought. Yet, she was rather grateful for the isolation since it gave her time to think. Of quietness, there was none. That was more than one could ask for on a train where kiddies reigned supreme. Johnny slept fitfully.

On arrival at the next stop, Helen was advised to stay over and await further developments, and again she was received with only the utmost kindness and sympathy. She and the flushed little boy were shown every possible consideration. Again she sent off a wire, this time asking for a reply. But again, none came.

Back on the train, she sat by her baby's bedside while he tumbled and tossed in troubled sleep. Her thoughts were a turmoil of uncertainty and doubt.

Had she not made a grave mistake? Should she not have stayed at home with Dad and Sue? Perhaps Bill was ill, in need of care. Perhaps he loved her no longer. Was there some embarrassment—or worse—in his past that he was unable to keep hidden? The conflict between love, trust, doubt, and anxiety was almost unbearable.

She remembered Bill in England, rushing here and there, papers in hand, signing this document or that, making sure— as far as he could—of her timely arrival in the Dominion. Had it all been a farce? She heard again his voice, full of happy assurance, picturing their bright future together. She heard again the songs of the West that he had taught her. The picture had been so glowing, so elaborate, that she had known it to be tinged with the aura of distance, with the blindness of homesickness.

She had been prepared for some letdown in the country itself, but never, never, in Bill. Bill of the bright, confident assurance. Bill of the broad shoulders and happy-go-lucky ways.

How proud he had been of their son! "Little Johnny Canuck" he had called him, promising that he should have a cowpony of his own one day—said he had the build of a farmer.

Then she remembered his last leave in England. He was home from Holland for ten days—confused by the traffic, irritable, frantic at the slightest noise, no longer interested in Johnny Canuck or anyone else—longing audibly for sunny Alberta as he sat gazing out at the rain-swept English countryside.

Helen had known the signs; battle fatigue, they called it. She was heartily glad when they shipped him home unexpectedly. Home to Canada and the West he loved so well. She had hoped against hope that the clear, clean air of the prairies and foothills he was so fond of would work a miracle of healing, and that he would find peace—find himself again.

His letters had given her small comfort, however, for they were few and forced, heavy with an air that was duty-bound. No mention of Johnny Canuck or a cowpony, they tore her heart. When she had written that she would soon be on her way "home" to Canada, there had been no reply at all. The silence was pregnant with misgiving and doubt for Helen.

"Oh God!" she prayed. "If there is a God who cares for little boys, then give his daddy back to mine."

When the train pulled into Edmonton, it was very late at night. Helen was dead on her feet, having kept going only by the strength of her determination. Her arms ached with the weight of the sleeping child. When the porter set her bags on the platform, she took her place beside them and stood there in a sleepy bewilderment. The crowd swarmed past her and gradually thinned, leaving at last only a few, all busy with their own affairs. No one was looking for a woman and a child, that was certain!

The loneliness—the terror—of a strange city swept over her. Near-panic gripped her. "Bill, Bill! How could you do this to us? Oh! Where are all your bright promises?" The cry rang through her heart, and she bent her head to look into the sleeping face of her child.

Feeling the pressure of a soft hand on her arm, she roused to see a kindly woman looking at her in concern. "I am the travellers' aid officer," she explained. "I can see that you are very tired. Can I phone someone for you? Get you a taxi, perhaps?"

"Where to? Where can I go?" There was frenzy in Helen's voice. "The only address I have is a small town north of this city. I had expected my husband to meet us here. I wired him."

There was an appealing winsomeness about the girl in her predicament, and the woman's heart went out to her. This, she was sure, was no ordinary case of upset plans, and the girl's English accent proclaimed her the bride of some returned soldier. "If you will come with me, I will get you something to eat. Then we can start phoning. Things always look worse than they are when it is night and one is tired. In the morning, you will see how much brighter the outlook is."

Helen thanked the woman for the comfort in her words and expressed the hope that she was right. She gladly gave the heavy child into the woman's arms. They soon found a taxi, and Helen was surprised to find that she was literally starved.

Having done full justice to a large and appetizing meal, she began to count the many circumstances in her favour.

She had a little money of her own—as much as she had been allowed to bring from England. It would be enough to carry her for a few weeks. She knew the Red Cross would exert every effort to help her locate her husband, and she had high hopes that once they got together, her love and understanding would help straighten out every difficulty. She had the names and addresses of several of the other brides who had been on the ship with her. She would phone them when she got around to it, but she knew better than to put much hope in voyage friendships. She had this friend beside her, this woman to whom she felt drawn in her dire circumstances. And she had Johnny! He was awake now and chattering happily on their new friend's knee.

Mrs. Kennedy (who had by now introduced herself) found a telephone and, while Helen waited eagerly, tried to get a call through to the village of Moosewell, where Bill might be found. Helen's hopes were dashed to the ground as Mrs. Kennedy hung up the receiver and turned to explain. "The operator says Moosewell is just a wide place on the road with a general store, a garage, an elevator, and some other small buildings."

They found out too that the railway passed through Cross Town, several miles distant, and did not touch Moosewell at all. But a daily bus service ran through it and then on to Cross Town.

Though Helen cried herself to sleep that night, she did sleep soundly and awakened in the morning refreshed, feeling an upsurge of courage and hope within her heart. She planned to contact the Red Cross centre early and felt sure there would be word that Bill had been inquiring for her.

When that did not happen, she was still undaunted and determined to keep cheerful. Although Mrs. Kennedy advised her to rest for a few days, she secured a timetable and immediately arranged to go to Moosewell on the first bus leaving.

Seeing how determined the girl was to try to solve her problem, Mrs. Kennedy again came to the rescue and led her to a motherly person who would care for the travel-weary baby while Helen was gone.

So it was that Ma Kelly came into the lives of Helen and little Johnny. Ma Kelly lived down on the flats. She had a quaint three-room bungalow with a shed roof—more garden than house. The windows were gleaming; the curtains, crisp and white. The cheery coloured linoleum on the floor was waxed till it shone.

Ma Kelly was not rich but, to use her own expression, she was "comfortable." She always found enough to give a helping hand to those in need, as do most folks in like circumstances. She was tall and plump, her size seeming to dwarf the small house. A clean white apron covered her print housedress, and she had a ringing laugh.

Ma Kelly held out willing arms to Johnny, and together they went in search of that elusive-something dear to the hearts of children—a cookie.

Helen sat on the white painted chair in the kitchen and thought of Aunt Min. Somehow, though she and Ma Kelly had scarcely exchanged a dozen words, Helen knew that here—in this tidy little home in this big, rambling, strange city—she and Johnny had found a haven.

Chapter Three

"Yes, Ma'am! Yes, Ma'am! You bet I remember Bill McElroy. Yes, Ma'am. Growed up here, he did. Dad raised him on the homestead north of town here. Mother died when he was knee-high to a grasshopper. Hard times, they had. We all did in the hungry thirties, what with wheat 'round eighteen, twenty cents a bushel. Old man McElroy made a good job of the lad too—hard worker like himself and well-liked by everyone. He enlisted and went overseas when the old man died. Near broke his heart, I guess... losing the old man, I mean."

Helen let the fellow talk on. Having found a good listener for once, he continued, pausing only to take the wheat straw from the side of his mouth, turn it around, and begin chewing it at the opposite end.

"Came back home some many months ago. Grown tall and handsome he was, but painful thin and with a haunted look in his eyes, like so many of them have. Was making right for the old place, but I guess I stopped him when I told him there was folks on it. Turned over to the community for taxes it was, several years ago. Seems when he inquired, he was told soldiers don't pay no taxes, but he forgot the place was still in the old man's name.

"Everybody here lost track of him. You know, these lads never are good at writing. So after a while, the township claimed it, placed a family on it—a veteran. Man with a lot of little 'uns. I'm sure Bill could've done something 'bout it, but he just turned right 'round and disappeared again. My missus felt bad when I told her 'bout it. Said she'd have had a right good time feeding some flesh onto that boy's bones again.

"I'm holdin' some mail for him, and a couple of telegrams, hopin' someday he'll show up again. He will, you know. There's always been a McElroy in this country. He's the last of 'em.

"...You would like his mail, Mrs. McElroy? You don't say! Well, now. Look, maybe I shouldn't have been shootin' off my mouth the way I did. Hope I didn't spill somethin' I weren't suppos'ta. Here y'are, Ma'am—some letters and two telegrams."

The old fellow pressed Helen to come in and meet his wife, but she escaped with the light bundle of mail. Finding a little path that wound across country, she followed it to the bank of a small river and, sitting down at the foot of a willow tree, she re-read the letters she had written many weeks before.

This, then, was the reason there had been no reply from Bill! This, then, the reason for his grim discouragement. Returning home from war—the home for which his very bones had ached and yearned—sick and baffled, he found it gone. His no more! People he didn't know living in the house his father had built with his own hands, where he himself had been born. Strangers on the land that he and his father had wrought from a wilderness.

Helen's heart went out in love and yearning, and a new determination to find him and make his life happier was here. As she sat, now, at the foot of the willow, something similar to eternal serenity entered her soul. Her weariness seemed to evaporate, and she arose strengthened and encouraged.

Back in Edmonton, she laid out her plans before Mrs. Kennedy and Ma Kelly—to get in touch with the Department of Veterans Affairs and also the Directorate of Repatriation and the Red Cross. Surely one of them would aid in her attempt to find Bill. They might even have an address where he could be found. He most definitely would have had dealings with the Department of Veterans Affairs, if only to apply for gratuities and credits.... If he had bothered about them at all.

Ma Kelly and Mrs. Kennedy both agreed that the disposal of the McElroy place had been illegal and advised Helen to consult a lawyer. They gave her the names of several good attorneys. Helen, however, decided to first try to find her husband. An even more pressing task was to find a home where Johnny could be cared for while she went to work. She felt sure that employment would not be hard to find, and money was something she would need before too long. When she mentioned the subject to the two women, they exchanged knowing looks.

Mrs. Kennedy said, "I can borrow a crib from my daughter Louise—a good one with a drop side."

Ma Kelly turned to Helen. "You could sleep on the studio lounge in the living room."

Helen was deeply touched. Ma Kelly had offered the use of the lounge with some diffidence, but to Helen, who remembered so many nights in air-raid shelters, it seemed like luxury in comparison. Her eyes filled with tears, and Ma Kelly reached over to squeeze her hand.

After a dreary tour of official places and long waits in various offices, Helen was at last ushered into the presence of the counsellor for Veterans Affairs. The man seemed kindly in a detached, impersonal way, and after a lengthy discussion with him, Helen came to the conclusion that she alone would have to battle this thing out. If Bill was to be found and restored to a right state of mind, she must call on every resource she possessed.

How could she expect these men to realize how much it meant to Johnny and her? To them, she was just one of many deserted wives. "Fellow probably fled the deck for a very good reason," seemed to be their attitude—or, "No great hurry. He will show up one of these days."

One thing she did discover, to her great satisfaction, was that Bill was getting his gratuity cheques. He had been having them sent to General Delivery at the large post office in the city centre. That meant he had been eating, anyway. His reestablishment credits had not been touched, and though he was listed as an out-patient in the military hospital, he had continually failed to report. This, then, was her predicament: no other address than General Delivery was given.

Not yet baffled, Helen discovered by shrewd questioning on what day the cheques usually arrived and laid her plans. "Twenty days to wait," she thought. Longer, maybe, unless God was good to her and Johnny by bringing Bill forward of his own volition.

On the third day, she counted her small hoard of money. After setting aside enough for Ma Kelly to cover their board and lodging and care of Johnny, she found herself with a very narrow margin. Then she thought of her shabby clothes and the practically shoeless state of the baby. Daringly, she pocketed a sufficient sum for a little shopping and boarded a streetcar for the downtown section.

Helen found Canadian prices rather confusing and much higher than one paid for the utility garments at home. This circumstance made it all the more imperative that she find employment. She purchased a very plain woollen suit, a frilly blouse, and a neat pair of shoes—"without coupons," she rejoiced. Her hat, she was glad to find, was as fashionably ridiculous as any she could buy.

Donning the new apparel, Helen was pleased with how she looked in the mirror and how the new items complemented her lean, tall figure. Asking that her utility coat and shoes be sent home to the little house on the flats, she started out with superb confidence to find her way to the Selective Service offices.

As she walked along the main street, she noticed the rattling, swaying old streetcars pass. "Such old-fashioned trains," she thought. But as she crossed the intersection, she was almost dragged beneath the wheels of a swift, modern trolley bus. Helen soon came to know that this was typical of the cities of the West.

Edmonton was the centre of a huge farming district, yet it also housed large industries and a few mining projects, too. The houses were spread so far out into the country that whole districts were rural in atmosphere. Its people were cosmopolitan—drawn from every part of the globe—and on its streets, Helen passed Indians with moccasined feet, long braids, and stoic features. There were also the high-heeled cowboys with sweeping, large-brimmed hats and gaily-coloured shirts, walking snappily with the click of spurs. There was a dash of glamour to them that quickened Helen's pulse.

This was the West that Bill had spent hours describing. German, Italian, French, Czech, Ukrainian, Russian—all were here. Whole districts of them within the city limits, and all intermingling on the downtown streets. Chinatown lay in the east end, and a few Africans lived there, too. Japanese were restricted and kept on the move, but she recognized a few as she made her way along.

Arriving at the Selective Service office, after much unnecessary walking and many inquiries, she was processed past five different officials. The last one extracted from her that she had, in England, worked in a factory equipped with power–sewing machines and had made parachutes and other army equipment.

After much discussion with several of the other officials, Helen was given a little card with the address of a large garment factory where power-machine operators were needed and told to report for an interview. She asked for directions and was helped by a kindly clerk who took time to draw a map on the back of an envelope. By his map, Helen was able to reach her destination with little difficulty. Her smart appearance and confident air won attention, and she was told to report for work at eight o'clock the following morning.

Elated, and because the new shoes were beginning to pinch, Helen decided to head for home. On her way to the streetcar stop, she stepped into a small bakery in the middle of the block, intending only to buy some small treat for Ma Kelly and the baby. But she stood spellbound at the lavish display of iced cakes, buns, and biscuits—almost overcome by the luscious fragrance that drifted in from the kitchen at the back. Her eyes fastened on a chocolate cake filled with whipped cream, but she seemed incapable of action and just stood, staring.

Inside the store, a young lady came forward and asked, "May I get something for you?"

"Yes," gasped Helen, "that!" as she pointed to the chocolate cake. "How much is it?"

"Thirty cents, Madam."

"Thirty cents." Not much more than a shilling! "Give me some of those, and those too. And have you any ice cream? ...You have. I'll take some."

"Strange customer," the clerk decided—she was so easy to please, and yet she looked as though she wanted to weep.

Helen heard Mrs. Kennedy's voice as she walked up the narrow pathway to the neatly painted door that stood slightly ajar. As she stepped inside, she heard their exclamation and felt puzzled by the slight disappointment in their tone.

"Why, we bought you a dress this afternoon," Ma Kelly told her. "This little green one. Thought you could save your money and yet look smart for your new job when you get it."

"That is alright," said Mrs. Kennedy. "You'll need both a suit and the dress. The suit looks lovely on you, and very business-like."

Helen laughed. "I love the dress. How kind you are!"

The two women looked at her. Her voice had more sparkle in it than they had yet heard. They wondered at the change.

"We are going to have a party," Helen went on, dropping her parcels on the table. Then, with a rather self-conscious air, "You see, I've got a job. I'm to report at eight o'clock tomorrow morning. But where is my son? I've not seen him for hours."

"Johnny is with Dennis, playing in the garden at the back. I'll go call him," and Ma Kelly disappeared through the back door of the quaint house.

Helen's day in the factory began the following morning. The forewoman was a big, raw-boned woman with an accent strange to Helen, and her manner and voice were rough. She put Helen to work on heavy denim overalls. The slim, English girl was used to hard work, glad, and thankful for the opportunity to earn enough to keep little Johnny in comfort. The factory was modern and equipped with music to make the working hours seem less tedious. There were short stops mid-morning and mid-afternoon when all the girls left their machines, making for the recreation room where milk, pop, tea or coffee, and sandwiches or cookies were supplied for a minimum charge.

In spite of all, as closing time neared each evening, Helen felt her back aching and the weight of the heavy material telling upon her. Then, too, the longing for Johnny increased toward the end of the long day, and always, at any time through the day, there was a vague uneasiness and a fretting worry at their unwonted separation.

She worked with a will and at the end of the factory week was rewarded with an envelope containing sixteen dollars. The rough-voiced forewoman unbent enough to smile and tell her that she was doing very well, indeed, for a beginner and that if she kept up her speed and continued to work as hard, she would soon be making double that amount. This information astounded Helen, since sixteen dollars for her first week was more than she had hoped for in her wildest dreams.

She found many friends in the recreation room, though most of them were in the older, quieter group. Helen never failed to find deep interest in the variety of nationalities and personalities of her workmates. At the machine to her left sat Yvonne Leveque of the dark hair and darker eyes; a quick, fiery French-Canadian girl. Small, but nothing frail or undetermined about Yvonne. She had a gay laugh that rang out over the hum of the machines, and her head had a proud lift. Helen admired her immensely and unwittingly began to imitate some of her mannerisms, as strangers will in a strange land.

On her right sat Elsa Smidt, "Smitty" to all her friends. Indeed, the nickname was used so much that Helen at first

thought it was the girl's right name. Elsa was blond and of
stocky build. Raised in a German settlement, she had gone to
a school where the German language was spoken, and she still
spoke with a guttural accent. This, despite the fact that she had
been born in Alberta. Elsa, or Smitty as she was better known,
was more the foreigner than Helen, just newly arrived.

Helen tried to nourish resentment against this girl for
reasons of nationality, but failed dismally in the face of the
unremitting kindness ever-flowing toward her from her fellow
worker on the right. It was Smitty who came to her aid when
she had trouble with an unfamiliar machine. It was Smitty
who introduced her to the recreation room, Smitty who explained the mechanism of the punch clock, Smitty who took
her on a tour of the less-expensive shopping district when she
wanted to buy shoes and underwear for Johnny. Smitty, in
every way, was a friend in need and a congenial companion,
even to the extent of bringing eggs and butter "from the farm"
for Johnny after a weekend trip home.

Smitty lived in a one-room apartment, yet she was always
so clean and fresh, blond and starched, that she brought a
breath of country air into the factory with her. So it happened
that one evening, she returned to Ma Kelly's hospitable small
house with Helen to eat supper with them and to meet little
Johnny. Helen felt she could not bear to receive further favours
from the girl without first making some small return.

They were in a strange continent—the tall, slim, obviously English girl and her blond, blue-eyed, obviously German
companion—but no one made any remark (if they noticed).
For thus things are done in this new world, where animosities

are few and hard to nurture. Helen stopped to tell herself this many times in the progress of their strange friendship.

Chapter Four

Soon came the day when Bill's gratuity cheque was due, and Helen phoned the factory to excuse herself. Taking her stand early, as soon as the post office opened, she waited in the wide vestibule where she could keep an eye on the General Delivery window and see everyone who approached it. At first, the janitor eyed her most suspiciously. He was a bent, shrivelled old man who wielded a long broom in and out of the corners and along the spacious vestibule. Helen smiled at him tremulously.

He looked surprised and said, "Morning, Miss," and then hurried past. After a long interval, he came back and asked, "You waiting for someone, Miss?"

"Yes," she replied. "I may have to wait for some time, but wait I must. I hope you don't mind."

"Oh! Nothing to do with me, Miss. You'd be warmer if you stood by that there radiator. It's chilly this morning." He shuffled off again.

By noon, Helen's feet were aching. She was hungry, tired, and very thirsty, but her determination never failed. She would stay right there, she had decided. As the morning wore on and she attracted more attention, she became embarrassed. She stood so very quietly in her attempt to be as inconspicuous as possible, and soon she grew unaware of the curious glances, occupied fully with trying to keep a brave face despite her utter weariness.

At last five o'clock came, and then, as the wicket closed down on the General Delivery window, Helen dragged herself painfully to the streetcar and home.

Ma Kelly greeted her with considerable alarm. "Honey, you look beat. Did you work today, or are you sick? Maybe you're coming down with something."

Helen forced a smile. "All I need is something to eat and then sleep. How's my son? ...No, Sweetheart, Mummy can't lift you."

Johnny had grown plump and brown as a berry. He shared a sandpit and swing with the child next door, who was his constant playmate. Ma Kelly went out of her way to cook rich and nourishing food for her "war baby," as she called him, and confidentially told her neighbour, "I don't know what I did with myself before I had him to look after." Even his tantrums were cute to Ma Kelly, and Helen had more than a suspicion that he was beginning to be spoiled, but she was so thankful that she scarcely gave that aspect of the situation a thought.

Too utterly disappointed to eat much, she went early to bed while Ma Kelly flustered and worried over her. She soon drifted off into a deep, exhausted slumber.

The next morning she again took up her position in the post office lobby, soon lapsing into a state of daydreaming—

traffic being light and few people coming and going at that early hour to hold her attention. The bent, old janitor passed her
with a friendly smile. Helen was miles away in her thoughts,
suffering a nostalgia that, until now, she'd had very little time
to indulge in. Homesickness swept over her with poignant
memories of Dad and Sue.

Involuntarily, the tears welled up and blinded her momentarily, and when she blinked them back and could see again,
Bill was standing in front of her.

The astonishment written on his face would have been
laughable under less-tragic circumstances. They were both ab-
solutely speechless for some seconds, and then they each began
to ask questions rapidly at one and the same time.

Helen was surprised to find that her reaction was one of
relief, now that she would be released from that dreary vigil
in a public place. Unconsciously, she relaxed her nerves and
body. Some of the tension left her face, and she sighed. Then
she took Bill's arm and steered him toward the door before
answering any of his questions.

She led him on toward the café where she and Smitty had
lunched after a shopping tour and, secluded in a corner booth
in the almost deserted place, told him, "Now you are going to
answer some questions from me!"

A dark, frustrated look crossed his face, and Helen took
time to survey him while they drank coffee. The change in
him tore at her heart. She had never seen this man of hers in
civilian clothes before. He was painfully thin, and an ashen
pallor was in his face. No longer was there a challenging lift to
his shoulders, no bright confidence in his face. Instead, there

was an intangible something, an inscrutable expression she found hard to understand.

A dull fear gripped her, and a chill swept over her. Suddenly, she found it hard to express herself. No words would come to her lips. How could she talk to this stranger about the things so near to her heart? He said slowly, with difficulty, "Is.... Did you bring the baby with you?"

"He's at home with Ma Kelly." She did not realize how strange this would sound to him. As an afterthought, she added, "Here in Edmonton."

He looked startled, and she resented the fact that he showed no gladness at the information.

"I've been to Moosewell. I know about what happened there. But Bill! How could you do this to us—to Johnny and me? You didn't even write for your mail, and I had no other address. Besides, they can't claim your homestead at Moosewell. Something can be done, legally, about that. You can fight and get it back!"

There came a faint stirring of hope in his dark eyes, but it flickered and went out. The broad shoulders sagged more wearily. "They can't claim it?" he asked scornfully. "Well, they've done it!"

How could he tell her of the bitter resentment that had almost choked him when he returned—battle worn, sick in mind and body—to the only retreat he knew, repeating over and over, "Home. Home." The sound of his own footsteps had echoed the words as he trod the familiar sidewalk of the small town where he had grown up.

How could anyone even understand the baffled longing of a man who has lost his only home, the memory of which had sustained him through hell and back again? How could words picture for her his journey—down the path toward the creek and across it, the short climb up the grade to the opposite side—and the feeling, as his stomach somersaulted, when he had stood in the dusk and watched smoke curl up through the air from another man's chimney? The chimney that had been his! Could another ever know the hatred and bitterness that was his as he saw the figure of a man bend over the old chopping block—the stump of a huge tree that was now in the walls of the old log house—to split firewood, and as he watched the child on the swing that he himself had used as a child—where his own son should play and no one else's? The pony tethered in the pasture had no right there, but there it was.

He recalled his trek in the pale moonlight through the south forty, where the fall wheat was springing fresh and green, washed in silver in the eerie light. Not his wheat, not his land any longer. He scarcely remembered the manner in which he returned to the city.

In some vague way, he knew he had ridden in a truck—a heavy-lumber truck. He had not gone back to the hospital, so urgent was his desire to be alone, but had taken a room in a cheap hotel, eaten in cheap cafés (when he ate at all) and, so far, had been unable to rouse from the lethargy that had settled down upon him—rising late, lounging through the day, going to bed only when he was too exhausted to stay up. Unshaven, unkempt, uncaring—living within himself, he was the very shell of a man, calling for his gratuity cheques only out of necessity. Unable to plan, he did not know what to say in writing—hopeless, disillusioned.

"Helen!" he cried hoarsely. "Why did you come? I have no home for you and the child—no job, no hope of one. You were better off in England with your own people. Why didn't you stay there?"

Helen's lips were dry. "You have not ceased to care? There is no one else?" she almost whispered, her eyes hungrily searching his face.

"Not care? Someone else? No, Helen. Not that—believe me, but...."

Helen looked long and silently into the face before her. When at last she spoke, her voice was weighted with care and anxiety.

"You need rest," she said. But thought, "Love and cleanliness, too."

"Rest?" he echoed. "That's all I do these days. I have been doing nothing else."

"Where are you going now?" Helen asked.

"To the post office." He came back to the present with a start and groped in his empty pockets. "I must pay for the coffee we drank."

Helen pressed some money into his hand and said reassuringly, "I will get it back later."

It was later that day that Ma Kelly stood in the doorway, nervously twisting the corner of her apron as she watched Helen and Bill make their way through a break in the fence and call to Johnny, who was playing in the neighbour's yard.

She watched the man pick up the child and look deeply into the dark eyes so like his own. Johnny silently sized him up in the way that children do, and then screwed up his face to cry as he turned and reached out to Helen. "Wanna swing," he howled. "Don't like man. Wanna swing!"

Helen hushed him and warned Bill that he could not expect Johnny to remember his dad. "After all, he was only a baby and not old enough to recognize anyone when you last saw him. It will take time to get acquainted with him."

Ma Kelly shook Bill's hand with less than her usual enthusiasm, and Helen understood that the misgivings in her kind eyes were rooted in the fear of losing Johnny. Yet Helen knew that that, too, was inevitable.

She asked cheerily, "May I bring company to luncheon, Ma?" She continued coaxingly, "I know I abuse your hospitality, because even I was not expected home. But just this once—please?"

Ma was instantly her beaming self again. "I'm only too glad, my dear, and you know it. Any way that I can help you young people, let me know." She bustled off to the kitchen while they found a seat on the steps of the little house.

Strange how questions—piled up, unanswered, in the back of one's mind—suddenly evaporate when the opportunity for reply arrives. Helen had already begun to disregard the past, content only to know that for the present her prayers were answered and Bill was once more here by her side—for better, for worse, for whatever the future might bring for them both. That many difficulties remained unsolved, and that the road ahead inclined steeply, mattered not at all.

They romped with Johnny and wandered by the wide, slow Saskatchewan River. They consumed the excellent food Ma Kelly prepared for them and sat out on the steps while dusk fell. They heard the voices of children at play in yards nearby and the uproar that followed the swish of a bat and the crack of a ball in the park on the corner. This was their day!

When the evening lengthened into night, Bill returned again to the city, and Helen lay down to sleep, happier than she had been for many a day.

Chapter Five

*H*elen knew that the most important thing at the moment was the health of her husband and, by much persuasion, she extracted a promise from him to go one morning to the military hospital for a checkup. It was no surprise to learn, as a consequence, that he was slated for several weeks of bedrest and treatment.

This gave her time to search for living quarters for all of them, and the hunt began. Staying downtown after the factory closed, buying an early paper, she started a systematic search of the city—on foot, by streetcar, or by taxi to some remote part. Helen demanded very little. "Somewhere our small family could all be together," she pleaded. But it was like asking for a cool spring in the desert! Edmonton, with a population swelled far past the point of aggravation, had no place to offer for a penniless war bride, her invalid husband, and their small son.

It was then that Ma Kelly had a suggestion to offer. "Why not put an advertisement in the paper yourself, Honey? Use a box number or this address, as you have no phone. Let's think up a good ad, one that will attract attention. Maybe this would do: 'Quiet home badly needed for overseas veteran (soon to be discharged from hospital), wife, and small son.' We could try it, anyway."

"Good idea," agreed Helen. "If I don't find anything among the places I'm calling at tonight, in it goes for the morning paper."

One of the addresses on Helen's slip gave only a phone number, so she stopped in at the corner store and asked permission to use their phone. "Why, sure. Help yourself," she was told.

A sharp voice answered her ring, "Got any kids?"

"One small boy of almost two," Helen replied, but before she could complete the sentence, the phone clicked sharply and was cut off. "Why, that's criminal!" she stuttered, getting red in the face with indignation. "It has happened to me several times, now."

"I know, Missus, but it's practically hopeless if you have any little ones. We have our married daughter and her family living with us for just the same reason."

The next call was at one-half of a duplex house in a fashionable district. It was unfurnished and the rent was terribly high, but it was a house for rent. Helen travelled a long way through the fast-darkening streets and finally arrived at the address given. "This is one way of getting to know my way around the city," she thought good-humouredly. "I think I have been in every district by now."

A bright light burned above the doorway. Apparently, callers were expected. A stooped old lady came to the door. "You want to see the house?" she questioned in broken English.

"Oh yes!" Helen answered breathlessly, trying not to sound too eager.

"But first, you got children?"

"Yes, one very well-behaved little boy," Helen replied with a sinking heart.

"Sorry." The door closed softly, but relentlessly, in her face.

Just one more address on her list for tonight. The lady who opened the door told her brightly and cheerfully, "My dear, the rooms were rented an hour after the paper was out." Then something in Helen's tired face arrested her. "Would you like to come in and rest awhile? You look played out, my dear."

"No, thank you. I will catch the next streetcar on the corner and hurry home." Helen turned wearily away.

The responses in reply to the advertisement were encouraging at first. With hopes raised, Helen hurried home one evening, her day at the factory through. With no home-hunting to be done, at least for tonight, she ate supper and then carried Johnny out to sit on her lap in the rocker on the lawn. How she enjoyed the luxury of cuddling her little son, singing to him softly! This was wonderful leisure after the rush she had gone through since the hunt for a place to live had begun.

Soon, the baby closed his eyes and was off to the land of nod. Helen kissed the sweet, rosy lips and softly removed the dusty little shoes. Ma Kelly came through the screen door with a pan of water and towels. Gently, they shared the task of cleansing the tanned, chubby face and hands, the dimpled knees and tiny feet. The fair, curly head dropped back on his mother's arm, and he remained unaware of the loving ministrations being bestowed upon him by the two women to whom he meant so much.

"Clean dirt," Ma Kelly murmured.

"How'll we get his overalls off and his sleepers on without waking him?" wondered Helen. But this was managed and Johnny was soon safely in his crib.

Helen returned to the lawn to carry in the rocker. The evening was cooling off. Just as she reached the bottom step, a big car pulled up at the gate and a handsome business-like man sprang out and came through the gate. He touched his hat, "You have an ad in the paper about a house?"

"Yes, I have." Excitement flushed Helen's cheeks.

"My wife is in the car. We will drive you over if you would care to have a look at ours. You might possibly be interested."

Might possibly be interested! "I will be dressed and ready in a second if you will wait for me," and Helen turned quickly and ran up the steps and into the house. Entering the kitchen, she threw her arms around Ma and gave her a bear's hug. Then she danced round the kitchen ecstatically and laughingly powdered her nose before donning a hat and coat. "Got to make an impression this time—I have a feeling it is my last chance."

Ma Kelly shook her head and sighed. "Your hopes are up too high. It can't be. It just can't be. Things don't happen that way."

"Hey! What happened to my faithful encourager?" Helen inquired, but was gone without waiting for an answer.

The bungalow had a narrow strip of lawn in front and a wide swath of it at the west side, a plot of kitchen garden was hidden at the back, and a low white picket fence surrounded it all. A sprinkler was playing on the lawn, turning slowly in its orbit, leaving grass and flower beds bejeweled in its path. Helen gazed at the gray stucco walls—splashed and peppered with black and white, giving an appearance of Irish tweed. It was crowned with a green and red asphalt–tiled roof. Picturesque window boxes dripped with flowering creepers, and scarlet geraniums proudly raised their heads above them. There were lawn bowls too, with purple pansies and yellow nasturtiums. Double hollyhocks rose close to the walls. Asters and zinnias lent their charm to the flower-beds beneath the windows.

Helen stood before the house, silently drinking in the loveliness. She made no attempt to move up the path.

"Don't you want to see the inside?" they asked her. The wife smiled sympathetically. "There was a lot of hard work involved to bring the place to this condition, but we loved doing it. This is a corner lot, as you see, and when we purchased the site prior to building, we hauled several truckloads of junk away before we began excavating for the basement. I'm afraid it had become the neighbourhood's dumping ground for old tin cans, broken bicycles, and such."

"One would never dream it to look at the place now," Helen murmured.

"No. Well, as I say, it was a tremendous amount of work, and we are well aware that the wrong people in the place would soon neglect and ruin the flowers and undo all our work in a few weeks' time. That is why we are very particular; you will be able to give us references, of course?"

"I... well... you know, I just arrived from England a few weeks ago."

"Yes, I guessed as much when you spoke. But your husband?"

"In the hospital, as you know. Previous to that, while I was still in England, he had been living in a hotel, but I will get the necessary references for you." Helen squared her shoulders.

The living room was a dream come true, decorated in soft pastel shades and with a low fireplace that invited one to pull up a chair. Built-in bookcases lined one wall and wide, sunny windows another. There were cozy scatter rugs on the hardwood floor and deep chairs placed at inviting angles about the room. The chesterfield was dressed in a gay cretonne slip cover, and there were end tables, lamps, and a cabinet radio.

The house contained no dining room, but at the sunny end of the modernistic kitchen there was a breakfast nook surrounded by windows. This was the first of its kind that Helen had ever seen, and she was intrigued with its convenience and brightness.

"Why, one could develop a suntan while eating breakfast," she exclaimed, and they all laughed delightedly.

The kitchen was outfitted with built-in cabinets that had drawers and cupboards for every conceivable use. There was a long, low window above the sink that looked out over some flower beds. The white and chromium sink sparkled as though it had never been used. There was a white enamel stove and an icebox. The floor was a gay cherry red inlaid–linoleum that matched the trimming on the spotless white woodwork and the tie-backs on the dainty curtains.

They went from the kitchen to the bathroom, where a low, green-marble tub matched the other accessories. Helen had a vision of Johnny splashing and rolling in that tub at bedtime.

Next came the bedroom with its pegged maple furniture, rose carpet, and soft lights. "Of course, we will take our own bedding with us as, no doubt, you have your own. Ours are mostly wedding presents, anyway."

Helen wondered what they would say if they knew she had nothing, not even a sheet to grace the lovely bed. Helen had thought it too unfair to carry anything like that from the rationed, poverty-stricken isle and had brought only a very few gifts received at her wedding and the farewell party—all of them small but treasured because of the sacrifices they represented.

The tour ended, they returned to the living room, and there was an unhurried grace about the pair as they kept up a light conversation. At last, Helen turned to her host and, hesitant to dispel the pleasant illusion she was enjoying, somewhat fearfully said, "How much are you asking for the place?" Her throat went dry as soon as the question was out.

She was thankful when he answered frankly: "The Rent Control Board has fixed the rent at—er—sixty dollars a month, but we are asking another sixty for the use of the furniture which, I am sure you will agree, is not exorbitant—references of course being satisfactory. And then there is the little matter of a down-payment on the key; that is usually worth, shall we say, two-hundred dollars."

At sixteen dollars a week, Helen earned less than seventy dollars a month. Bill would get some kind of hospital allowance eventually, but Helen knew it would not be nearly enough. Then the money for the key; that was a stickler. And there would be meter fees and deposits to the city, no doubt. It was all far out of her reach.

She shook her head and smiled at them both. "Well, it was a nice dream while it lasted."

This was what they had half-expected to hear, having a fair idea of a returned-man's resources, so they were very understanding and said rather apologetically, "You know, we will be up against something of the same situation when we arrive at the coast, where we have been transferred."

"Only," thought Helen, "your purse will be well-padded, and you will probably know people and have some pull through business associations." When the door had closed behind her, she stood to look at the sprinkler playing on the lawn and she imagined Bill and Johnny romping there through days of sunny weather—Bill grown brown and carefree, strong and well again.

The next day at noon at the factory, Helen broke through the innate reserve and shyness that had kept her mainly a listener until now. She entertained the girls around her table in the recreation room with a minute description of the lovely little dream-bungalow. All the longing, frustration, and home-hunger throbbed in her voice, and the girls sat enchanted. When the tale was finished, there was a short silence before one of the girls spoke up.

"Do you know what I would have done?" she said. "I would have taken the bungalow, paid them for the key, then gone to the Rent Control Board and sued not only for the return of the two-hundred dollars but for damages too. The shysters!"

"Oh, you would, would you?" another spoke. "Well, let me tell you—innocence personified—that they don't give receipts in such instances, and how would you have proved your claim? We had to pay eighty dollars for some awful rugs that were called 'floor covering' in our contract. They were so old that the first thing we did when we moved in was tear them up and throw them away, but if we had not been willing to swallow the bait, others would, and we were desperate for a place to live. We would even have paid a bonus for the cockroaches they'd left us—free of charge."

"Helen," began Smitty hesitatingly, "there's—I happen to know—a furnished suite that will be vacant soon in the basement of the house in which I live. No one else knows, but Inga Pederson—she is a Dane and as clean as can be—told me they were going back to the farm to help her mother and father, who are getting too old to manage by themselves. I asked her not to tell our landlady yet until I talked it over with you. There are only two tiny rooms, and even they are down in the basement. Inga has one child, so surely Mrs. Carlson will not object to Johnny. The rent is low—only twenty-five a month."

Helen opened her purse and counted her money. "Twenty dollars and thirty cents. I can get some more from Bill. How much more will I need? You count dollars and cents much quicker than I."

"Four dollars and seventy cents, and there is a fifty-cent charge for the use of the phone. Better pay it. It saves street car tickets in the end. Look, Helen, I can let you have the money, and if you come home with me tonight, we will go to Mrs. Carlson about it. She is a tough customer, but not as bad as some, and if she happens to take a liking to you, you get the breaks."

After the factory hours that night, Helen saw Smitty's tiny bedsitting room for the first time. Here a couch by day folded down to a bed by night; in its daytime state it was a cushioned lounge. Here a closet turned out to be a kitchenette, fitted with an electric stove. Shelves for dishes, a cupboard for food. Here a small window box, nailed precariously, must satisfy one's love of the soil; such a love lay deep in the heart of Smitty.

Smitty led Helen along a clean, polished hallway and pointed to a doorway. "This is the bathroom," she explained. "Twenty-one people in this house share it, so when we are through, we leave the door open. That way we can always tell when it is unoccupied."

After supper, the girls walked down some wide steps and entered a large, square room in the basement. In the corner stood the large hot-air furnace, unused at this time of year. Near it were stationary washtubs and a copper washing machine.

"This is the laundry, and it costs twenty-five cents every time you use it. I just wash my few things out in the bathroom, although that's not really allowed. It would pay you, with a family, to use it once a week."

Smitty next knocked at a door, which was opened by a small, fair girl who held a chubby boy in her arms. Wiping his mouth as she spoke, she said, "Oh, hello Smitty. Is this your friend you were speaking to me about?"

"Yes. Helen wanted to get everything settled as soon as possible. Helen, this is Mrs. Pederson; Inga, Mrs. McElroy."

Helen nodded gravely, and Inga smiled.

"It is not much of a place, Mrs. McElroy, but if you are anxious, as we were, to find somewhere to live, you won't care. We had a lovely apartment, once, in the west end, but when the owner of the place discovered I was expecting a baby, she made our life a living hell-on-earth to force us to move—shut off the heat, insulted our visitors, grumbled and complained until I became ill and terrified. I knew how impossible it would be, once the baby arrived, in that ultra-exclusive place, where a baby's cry at night would startle them out of their super-refined wits and the sight of a diaper on the line would shock their sensibilities. So Cornelius walked the streets, knocking at doors, until he found this place. Now, we wonder why. My folks wanted us on the farm even then, but Cornelius had an in-law complex."

"Well, it's lucky for me you have made up your mind just now. I wish we had a farm to fall back on, and someday, maybe we will. In the meantime, I, like you, am thankful for small mercies. If I can persuade Mrs. Carlson to let me have this place, I will be very glad, for I'm worn out working through the day, house-hunting at night, and dashing off to the hospital at every odd moment. If Ma Kelly were not so dependable,

Johnny would feel like a little orphan. Smitty, too, has been a real friend."

"If you will both sit down, I will fix a bottle for my son and put him down in his crib. Then we can go up to Mrs. Carlson. She has no idea that we plan to leave. We kept it quiet, Smitty and I."

Mrs. Carlson looked surprised when she opened her door and saw the three girls facing her. "What's wrong now?" she demanded, looking straight at Smitty. "Some more complaints?"

"No! No! Mrs. Carlson," Smitty hastened to quiet her, "we have something important to ask you, and we want you to meet our friend, Mrs. McElroy."

"Oh!" She gazed directly at Helen with a piercing glance, then stepped back and said, "Come in. No need to stand out in the hall."

Once inside, Inga began timidly, "Mrs. Carlson, Mrs. McElroy was wondering if you had a suite to rent." Growing red in the face, she gulped.

"No, of course I haven't, and you know it!"

"We thought one might be coming vacant soon, and you might give her first chance," urged Smitty.

"Well, I don't know of one, but if somethin' should come up, I'll let you know." This was said with an air of dismissal.

"We... uh... we might be leaving in a few weeks for the farm, and we hoped she could have the suite we are in, Mrs. Carlson," stuttered Inga.

"Oh! Is that the idea?" Then slowly, "Well, it's twen'y-five dollars a month, paid in advance. And another thing—have you any kids? I've made up my mind I ain't goin' t'have any more brats wakin' me up nights with their howlin'.'"

"Oh, is that so? I suppose you came with a full set of teeth and never wore diapers. You.... You are the kind of people my husband has lost almost everything for, including his health. Fighting... for you! You are the kind of people the boys were protecting through six years of hell. You black-market money grabbers who have the upper hand over veterans and their families.

"Well times will change, and I will work to make them change. This great country, this free country, blighted... by things like you!" Helen was surprised at herself, but she was much too burnt up about it all to care. She was defending Johnny and, in some vague way, Bill and every other war veteran. Every instinct of motherhood was well up in arms at the hard-boiled attitude she had encountered.

"If I have to walk to Ottawa with a picket on my back, I will bring this thing out into the open. It is disgusting. And who are the sufferers? The young men and women who were denied their happiness in the years of the depression, who were parted for years because of war service and now have small sons and daughters around them. Yet still, they are denied normal family lives... and by people like you who sat at home in comfort, piling up bank accounts."

Helen was magnificent as she stood with her head thrown back, her eyes flashing—indignation in every spoken line—proud and unafraid.

"I will go to see a lawyer to find out if we cannot legally sublet our suite to whomever we please." Inga stamped her small foot, incensed by the remark about brats.

"Well, now." Mrs. Carlson was taken aback. "No one told me your husband was a veteran, did they? There are lots of English people in this burgh. Give me time to think this over. How many youngsters have you? ...Oh, one—that's not bad. Have you seen the suite? Did you say twen'y-five was a'right?"

"I have the money here right now—twenty-five dollars, and fifty cents for the use of the telephone—and I would like to use the laundry every week. I will pay for that when I use it."

"You're a smart one, ain't you?" There was a tone of un-willed admiration in her voice as she took the money and reached back for her receipt book. "About the black market, Mrs. McElroy. The prices of my suites are fixed by the Rent Control Board, and the price includes the use of the furni-ture."

Smitty found it hard to keep her face straight as she re-membered the battle of the Rent Control Board—Tenants vs. Owner. But for Helen, the battle of house-hunting was over for the time being.

Chapter Six

*I*t would take Inga almost two weeks to wind up her affairs and get ready to move back to the farm, and her rent was paid up until that time.

Helen planned to have Bill come home as soon as she was ready to move in. He would be unable to work for some time, and in the meantime, he could care for Johnny during the long days while she worked at the factory. He would be able to draw an outpatient's allowance until he was well enough to work, and between them, they could make their expenses. Helen planned to strictly budget her housekeeping money to save enough for legal expenses, if they were necessary, in the fight for the McElroy homestead.

Ma Kelly was genuinely thankful to know that the young couple was getting a start once again, but her kind old heart almost broke at the thought of losing her small companion. "Could you not leave him here with me through the week while you are working?" she pleaded. But Helen had found it so hard to part with him, even during the day, and she waited so anxiously for evening to come when she could get home to hold him in her arms again.

"Ma, I couldn't," she said with tears in her eyes. "I see so little of him as it is."

"You will take time at nights to cook his custards and soups, won't you? I'm so afraid you will have him eating out of cans all the time. Now come, let's write the recipes down. Here is the way I cook his cereal in a double boiler." She was forcing a cheerfulness so that she might not dampen Helen's bright happiness.

Bill's condition was improving, and he began to get passes that allowed him to leave the hospital for a few hours at a time. He visited the small home on the flats and painstakingly tried to win his small son's confidence. It was not a difficult task, for the child had a naturally happy and friendly disposition, and an utter trust in the goodness of the world. It was not many days before he came to be the small shadow of the tall, wilted young man with the gray pallor and the burning eyes.

In the evenings, Helen would sit and watch them quietly. It dawned upon her in a dreadful realization that Bill's interest in the rollicking boy was forced—that there was a pathetic urgency in the earnest effort that he made to keep his attention on the demanding child. Slowly she formed a grim resolution, and several days later she climbed the stairs leading to the office of the chief medical officer.

Seated across the desk from the serious-eyed medical man, she looked directly into his face and said, "I came to see you about my husband, Doctor. I cannot help feeling worried. I am not satisfied with the progress he is making."

"I'm sorry to hear that, Mrs. McElroy. I'll ring for the files if you will just wait—much easier to discuss a patient with the charts at hand." He pressed a button as he spoke. A smart young nurse appeared immediately and then disappeared to return quickly with a file, which she placed before the doctor, and she again withdrew. He opened the file and studied its contents for a while in silence. Helen saw the expression on his face grow more grave, more serious. Then he looked across at her.

"You know, don't you, Mrs. McElroy, that we have your husband under the care of a neuro-psychiatrist?" he questioned.

"No, I did not, but I would have ventured the suggestion myself if you had not, Doctor."

"His progress has been unusually slow, and we have been unable to discover the reason in view of the facts that he suffered no major wound and that the small wounds to his head and leg have healed perfectly, scarcely leaving a scar and no disability. You are right in thinking he has shown little improvement, despite the fact that we have done the utmost with modern science and drugs. At present he is receiving mental therapy. However, we have high hopes that now you are here, you will be able to make a home for him and a more favourable environment."

"That, too, was one of the subjects I wanted to discuss with you. I have been able to find a small, very inadequate apartment—but it is an apartment—and I plan to continue working at least a few days every week to bolster our income. I had hoped that Bill would be able to care for our two-year-old boy for part of the time. Do you think that would be advisable?"

"If he is fond of the child, a good idea—a very good idea. The responsibility may be just what he needs. I would suggest you carry out your plans. The child would be quite safe with your husband, too—unless his condition gets worse."

"Gets worse?" Helen was alarmed at the thought. "Doctor, please explain to me further. What symptoms must I watch for? How would I know?"

"Well, it would be most inadvisable to do any watching so that he would notice. You must show every sign of confidence and unconcern in order to help him regain a grip on himself. A lot will depend on you. However, for your benefit, there is no danger unless the patient begins to show periods of mental blankness, increased failure to concentrate, or even loss of memory."

"Danger of what, Doctor?"

"Now, Mrs. McElroy, there is no need for alarm at this point. I feel sure that your good sense and the fact that you have the beginnings of a home together—not to mention your love and understanding, which I presume—will be what Bill needs. These things are, to me, of great value today. If at any time there is need for further discussion, we will get together again. And I wish you every success in your efforts; you really deserve it."

Helen rose and made her way to the street. Her feelings were mixed. There was quiet assurance in her own ability to meet the conditions and a faith in the memories of the Bill of old, but also a faint premonition of grief ahead.

The day they moved into the tiny basement suite was a gala occasion for all but Ma Kelly, who wept silently into the suitcase she filled with little shirts and overalls, socks and shoes. She hugged the baby tight, then watched the taxi longingly until it was out of sight.

Helen's lip trembled as she said, "Remember, Ma, I'm counting on you to look in on my family occasionally while I'm at work."

"Honey, I wish you didn't have to work. Both of those boys need a mother!"

"I know, I know, Ma, but it won't be for long."

The days at the factory seemed longer now, so constantly was her mind on the problems at home. Bill's weary face rose up before her as she stitched the long seams up the sides of overalls. Smitty was an increasingly dear friend and the devoted slave of little Johnny.

Helen worried about the money she spent on tiny socks, shoes, novelty print shirts, and gaily-coloured overalls. She vied with Ma Kelly, who came over frequently and opened her shopping bag to produce his favourite cookies, fresh eggs, or a jar of homemade jelly. "Are you sure he's getting enough to eat? He looks pale to me," she fretted.

Helen did notice that the roses in his cheeks were fading, and she coaxed Bill to take him in his little red wagon to a child's playground each morning in the early sunshine. This was scarcely sufficient to make up for the long hours he had spent on the lawn or in his sandpit in the garden at the flats.

However, the apartment house opened its front door right onto the street and the sidewalk of a busy thoroughfare. There was not a sign of grass or a place to play for several blocks. Bill, too, needed the outdoor exercise, but Helen comforted herself with the thought that the days were shortening and getting chilly, and as winter approached there would be more inclination to stay indoors and keep warm.

Helen's days were packed to the brim, as she rose very early in the morning to dress the baby, feed him, and clean the two rooms before she went off to the factory at eight o'clock. She lived nearer now and had a few extra minutes at home. Bill managed lunch for himself, and Helen urged him to see that he and Johnny both drank lots of milk. She propped the high windows open, but the air that descended to the tiny rooms was dusty.

Bill spent the greater part of every day flat on his back on the bed in the bedroom, and Johnny romped and rolled over him or fell asleep in the crook of his arm. Together, they certainly had enough rest.

They soon became unconscious of the noise and movement—necessary in a household of so many people—and grew into a little world of their own, consisting of the three of them, Ma Kelly, and Smitty. They occasionally saw other tenants, speaking briefly in the hallway before passing on. Mrs. Carlson bothered them not at all, so long as Helen kept the rent paid up regularly.

Truly—a big city can be the loneliest place in the world.

Ma Kelly's faithful ministrations were unceasing, and the trips Johnny made with her to the downtown shopping centre were the highlights on his narrow horizon. He looked forward, eagerly, to the tours of the big department store where Ma shopped for herself and sometimes picked up groceries that Helen had asked for.

Johnny liked to stand back and watch the fine spray of cool water as it descended on the counters of fresh vegetables. He liked the bright colours of the fruit on display in great variety. He sniffed contentedly at the fragrance that drifted around the cookies and cakes, knowing that Ma never failed to produce a cupcake or some such dainty after a visit to this department. He waited his turn at the candy counter and pointed out his choices with implicit faith that they would be forthcoming. Yet with manly disregard, he gave not a glance at the counters where suits and overalls were shown, caring very little—in the way little boys have—of the way he was dressed, so long as he was warm or cool as the season demanded.

Bill was thankful, too, for the relaxation this afforded him from the constant responsibility of caring for the child. He began to look forward, with affection, to Ma Kelly's frequent visits, and he missed her cheerful smile on the days she did not appear. He took his duties of child care very seriously and carried out every detail with an intensity of concentration that brought him to near exhaustion.

Helen typically came home shortly after five o'clock in the afternoon and prepared a good, balanced meal, dusted and tidied as it cooked, and took pains to serve the meal with interest in order to coax Bill's jaded appetite. Then she would relax and talk over the day's events while they washed and dried the dishes together. After that, they usually romped with Johnny or took him for a little walk around the block before putting him to bed. He was bathed and tucked in for the night, after which came mending, washing, or even ironing.

On rare occasions there was time to read to, or with, Bill. They shared a love of good reading. Once in a while, Smitty would offer to stay with Johnny while they went off to a movie or hockey game or church service together. Helen began to feel the need of warmer clothing as winter came on and the temperature dropped, but she was hoarding away every nickel with a bigger project in mind.

Bill went two or three times to the outpatients' ward of the hospital. On those days, Ma took over where Johnny was concerned.

With winter's approach, the days grew shorter, the hours of bright sunshine lessened, and it was necessary to keep the windows closed and the electric light burning all day in the dark rooms. The noise of Mr. Carlson tending the furnace at regular hours was added to the other noises of the house, and it wakened them early in the morning and late at night.

The closed windows and the proximity of the big furnace had a peculiar effect on Bill. He felt imprisoned and suffocated, and the resultant fretfulness and irritability worried Helen, although she was unaware of the cause as Bill did not complain openly—nor could he have even expressed himself very clearly on the subject, had he tried. She was aware only that Bill was more restless, less contented. The burning in his dark eyes pulled at her heartstrings, leaving her uneasy and disturbed.

Late one afternoon, the factory door opened and the girls streamed into the street, which was already darkening. The chilly north wind struck through the thin coat and sweater Helen was wearing, and it tore at her bare legs and hands. She put one hand up over her ear, but quickly pulled it down again and tucked it inside her coat. The streetlights came on suddenly, brightening the bleak aspect a little as she made her way along.

"If this is a fair sample of Canadian winters, I can see I am going to have to buy some warmer clothing, like it or not. That is, if I am to continue going out to work every day," she said to Smitty, who hurried along at her side.

"I think Ma Kelly is right; you should try to stay at home for a while. Bill looks worse instead of better, lately, and I get worried about Johnny. I know Ma does, too."

"I have made up my mind to quit at the end of the month. You know we get the outpatients' allowance, and I think if I were to budget strictly, we could manage, but.... Oh Smitty, I have a fear of almost getting the homestead back and then losing it for want of a lawyer's fee or some such thing."

"I know it is a lot of responsibility when you are so alone," sighed Smitty.

As they opened the door of the rooming house and stepped into the dim hallway, a strong odour of insecticide mingled with that of cooking flooded Helen as she passed the doors of the different apartments on her way down to the basement. As she entered her own little apartment, Bill was bending over the stove, where something bubbled merrily. Johnny sat in his highchair, banging on the tray with a spoon. "Soup, soup,

soup, soup," he sang a little song. But on Helen's entrance, he changed it to, "Mummy, Mummy, Mummy, Mummy."

"Hello, Mummy's darling." Helen kissed him and tumbled his curls. "How goes the day's battle, Daddy?" she asked, turning to Bill. "Mmm! Smells good. Better than what the Brownses or Carlsons had when I passed their doors."

Bill's eyes were heavy as he nodded his head without speaking. Helen had already tied an apron around her waist as she said, "Let me take over here, Darling. You lie down for a while. I'll fix the table and then call you."

Bill went into the bedroom and flung himself down on the bed, face down, head on his hands. Helen followed him to the bedroom door and watched him for a few moments, a tiny frown creasing her brow. Then, turning slowly, with heavy steps she went back to the stove.

When she roused Bill, with gentle hands rumpling his hair, she said softly, "Come on, Lazybones. Your son has had his supper and bath and is asleep. Come, let's you and I eat, honeymoon style."

Bill rolled over on his side and grasped her hand, then held it tight. "You are pretty swell people, Helen," he told her huskily. "I want you to know it, to know that I know it—pretty swell people. I don't like to see you working so hard. Wish I could be of more help to you."

"The biggest help you can be to me, Darling, is to get well."

"I wonder. I am only a drag, Helen. I can't even help myself."

"Why, Dear, you were doing so well only a few weeks ago. I was all hope and ambition for you."

"I know, Helen, but... it's... it's this being underground all day. People walking around over my head. No air, no sunlight. Oh, Helen, sometimes I get the feeling I'm buried alive."

"That's better, Bill. It is always better to talk things over. Get a load off your chest somehow. Oh, Bill, I may have something to tell you very soon."

He looked at her with a puzzled look in his eyes while dragging himself off the bed and out to the little table. Helen poured tea and placed some food on his plate.

"I'm ravenous even if you aren't, and this is a very good stew you made. Where did you learn to cook, Bill? You're not hiding a past from me, are you? Who was your instructress?"

"Why, Dad taught me. Dad was the best cook in the North, once. His sourdough hotcakes were something to wake up to—or dream about—and his venison stew.... Well, I couldn't get venison, of course, but I was able to get a nice piece of veal. We didn't need coupons in those days, Helen. Why, the game walked right into our homestead; we didn't even have to hunt them. Dad used to say—jokingly, of course—that we shot them in self-defence. The first well that was dug in the town became a trap for a yearling moose who fell into it one night. That's why the place is called Moosewell."

They ate in silence for some seconds. Then Bill continued, "His moose steak—and he had a special way of broiling it— made one hungry only to sniff its aroma while it was cooking. I've eaten bear steak too, and the way Dad cooked it, it was good! Dad made pies with bear grease for shortening, and they were tender and delicious—or else distance gilds my memory. He would hunt down a bear in the fall—prime with the ripe berries it had devoured all summer long—and render the fat to store away. Then we would enjoy gooseberry pie, saskatoonberry pie, blueberry pie, and rhubarb pie all winter long."

"But berries don't grow in the winter, Bill."

He looked at her with blank astonishment. "We picked them in summertime and fall, and put them into glass sealers to preserve them."

"Who? A man and a boy?"

"But of course. You should have seen our house. Dad kept it as clean as any woman could—cleaned windows and scrubbed floors. When I brought him home bouquets of wildflowers— wild lupine, Indian paintbrush, or even dandelions—he put them in empty sealers on the living room table. A home for me; that was what Dad wanted, and he made it, too."

"In the winter, Bill, when the crops were in and the hay was stacked, then what?"

There was a hush in Helen's voice and her eyes were moist. This was the Bill who had won her heart back there in England. Bill, with his fine loyalties and enthusiasms. The Bill who had drowned out the sound of the sirens with word-pictures of the other life he knew. And instinctively, Helen knew that once again Bill was painting out the present with memories of the happy past. As he spoke, the reality of the two small rooms receded, and he was once again in the rambling log house with the huge barrel heater. Again he lay upon the wolfskin on the floor, while his dad told him how he 'bagged' it on the trapline, how Jimmy Blackcrow had taught him how to tan it, and how Mother had been more frightened than surprised when she had unwrapped his gift. She had thereafter pictured the trapline as a place of terror, haunted by gray wraith-like figures that hunted down her man.

"You don't remember your mother very well, do you, Bill?"

"Yes, I do, and Dad brought her back to me so vividly when he spoke of her. My real difficulty now is to recognize the real memory from the tales that were told.

"In those early days, when Mother was alive, the pioneers literally lived off the land and fought for existence through the grim, snowbound winters. When the crops were in and the hay stacked in the sluice, where it had been cut, we fenced it around to keep the wild game away and left it there to be hauled home on the snow. But we were still not finished. The log buildings had to be chinked against the cold winds of winter, roofs mended if need be, and corrals fixed for the cattle.

"Then, when Indian summer was over and the snow came down to blanket the trails sufficiently, we rose before the sun in the morning, and after a good breakfast of mush, home-cured bacon, and sourdough flapjacks, we would stoke the big barrel heater with a chunk of half-green cordwood and shut off all the drafts. That kept it burning slowly, and the house would be warm when we got home again.

"Then we'd light our lantern and, buttoning up our mackinaws—our earflaps down and thick mittens on our hands—we would go out to the barn."

Bill was silent for a moment as the smell of the barn, from the horseflesh it sheltered all night, came back to him through the years.

"The air would turn to a sort of mist in the light of the lantern as we opened the big, heavy door and let the frosty air come in. Then we would harness Bet and Bob. They were chunky dapple grays, colts from the same mother. Dad raised them in our barnyard. Hitched to the sleigh they made a fine team. We would follow the old-wood road up over the hill that Dad had cleared when he first homesteaded there.

"There were no proper roads in those days, just wagon and pack trails. But Dad had cut this road out of the bush in the early days and had put it to constant use. We still used it for a wood road until I left home. It followed the creek for a little while and then turned and climbed a hill, going up and over the ridge to drop again, cross a creek, and then up a smaller hill, down again to the lakeshore. There was a good stand of timber on the near shore in those days, though it has been cleaned out now for many a day. On the lakeshore, we would fill our sleigh with logs if we were building or poles if it was a corral we had in mind. We picked dry wood if the haul was for firewood.

"Eating our lunch on the lakeshore was the part of the day I loved the best. Dad taught me how to keep still and make friends with the squirrels and chipmunks, and I loved the taste of the coffee boiled in an old lard pail or syrup can. Somehow it smelled of pine cones and spruce needles and tasted like nectar to me. I would fill my pocket with the pine cones, but when I got home, I found they had lost their magic of the outdoors.

"Coming back, the trail would be frozen hard, and the sleighs—loaded down with heavy logs—would screech as they went along, and Dad would sing, his voice coming back in the form of an echo from the bush. I was never afraid, and the shadows of the tall trees in the snow seemed like people I knew. I felt good out there in the moonlight. When we reached home and swung the big door open, the warmth of the house was like a friendly benediction to our day in the open."

Helen was quiet, loath to break the silence when Bill had stopped speaking. At last she said, softly, "You remember all that, Bill—so clearly, so distinctly."

Bill looked up, startled, for hers had been the same thought as his.

"Yes, Helen." There was a plea for understanding in his tone. "I can remember all that, and plainly. But those days—the days in England when I first knew you, when I told you I loved you and married you and promised you a future and a home here in Canada.... Oh, may God forgive me! They are full of shadows in my memory. My little son, who wears my face today... I can hardly recall him at all. Though believe me, Dear, I love you both! But the things that happened before Normandy are just dull etchings in my mind, hidden behind the blanks—the dark places in my mind where I cannot, where I dare not, look.

"I force myself to recall incidents and details. When you speak of your father and Sue—I'm sorry, Helen—I can scarcely remember them at all. They come up before me in the night—not the memories, but the blanks—and my mind goes searching; my nerves are screaming. God, Helen, I'm afraid to remember, even if I could!

"There is something there, behind the blankness, that is pulling and tugging, and it is blighting my life. Nothing seems real because of it, except my life before the war. It seems as though this life, in these two rooms, is a dream that will come to an end. As if I will wake up and be back there again. And I live for that promise."

Tears streamed down Helen's face as she went back to the old subject of their conversation. "How about school, Bill? You must have gone to school."

"Most surely I did—on Peg-legs. We called her that because she was so very long-legged. A tall, graceful sorrel mare. A fast walker, too. We made good time on those four miles to town. Dad made my lunch and packed it in a pail—ground meat sandwiches and pickles, an apple or a carrot, thick oatmeal cookies. Miss Johnston made us some hot cocoa, for which we took turns at bringing milk.

"In cold and stormy weather, Dad taught me at home. And the winter that I fought with measles and whooping cough, I didn't go to school at all, but I studied the correspondence course for grade five and passed into grade six at the end of the year. Dad was a proud man that year. It was as though he, himself, had won some coveted degree."

Supper over, they washed and dried dishes together. Helen attacked the pile of washing, leaving it rinsed and starched, ready to be hung on the line early the next morning before she left for the factory. Then she wrapped a few sandwiches for her own dinner and prepared a casserole for the oven, which Bill could cook with very little trouble.

Finally, she switched off the light and crawled in beside Bill—lying there, by his side, in the darkness. Helen felt aware of his tenseness, and she knew he was wide awake. She was very weary after her long day, but she raised her steady hand to smooth the wrinkled forehead of the sleepless man. He folded his hand over hers and seemed to relax. Presently Helen was in a deep sleep of physical and emotional exhaustion.

She wakened with a start and a premonition of something wrong and found Bill's place beside her was empty. The bed covers were turned back cornerwise, and his folded clothing gone from the chair beside the bed. Helen realized she must have slept for some time.

She sat up, raising her hands to her face in bewilderment and horror. Suddenly she felt helpless and alone, uncertain what action to take. She got up, put on her housecoat, and began pulling on her shoes, impatient with herself over the fear that oppressed her. Yet the doctor's warning had ever been just beneath the surface of her mind, and now it came up to confront her. "If his condition gets worse..." he had said, and Bill was definitely a sick man lately.

The noise wakened Johnny, who pulled himself up by the side of his crib, crying loudly and with all the indications that he meant to keep it up. Soon there came a thumping on the ceiling as the tenants above protested the disturbance so early in the morning.

There was nothing Helen could think to do about Bill. No plan would formulate in her tired brain. Taking Johnny in her arms, she slipped off her shoes and climbed back onto her bed. She held the convulsive little body close to her own until his sobs quieted down. Johnny returned to the land of baby dreams before she returned him to his crib.

For Helen, however, there was no further sleep. She lay in the darkness, every nerve alert, listening to the sounds in the over-crowded house. She heard the house door open and close and became aware of heavy steps making their way slowly along the hallway, down the stairs, and through the tiny kitchen in the darkness.

"Bill?" Her voice was scarcely above a whisper.

"Are you awake, Helen?" He switched on the light. "I'm sorry, Darling. I couldn't stand it any longer. There was no air in the room. Outside, the air is sparkling clear at this time of morning. The streets are quiet, and they look clean and wholesome in the moonlight. Dawn is just coming up over the chimney tops, and the first milkmen are beginning their deliveries. I thought I would get back before you wakened and missed me."

He brought the fragrance and coolness of fresh air into the room with him, and Helen understood a little of his longing and heartache. He sat on the edge of the bed and held her close, running his fingers through her hair. "You need the country, Bill—your farm. We will go there in the spring. Have patience, Darling."

"Yes, Honey. Yes, we will." There was disbelief in his voice. His eyes lacked confidence.

Bill and Helen grew closer together as weeks lengthened into months. It was like the building of a new life and love, rather than the renewing of the old. To Bill, the past was something to be avoided—even in one's thoughts—but he was touchingly grateful to Helen for her faithfulness and love for him. Even his small son won for himself a place of deep affection in the heart that was so full of shadows. Weary weeks dragged on, and winter at last gave promise of spring.

With the sunny days of February and the lamb-like weeks of March, Bill's restlessness grew. With the lengthening of the days, Helen's fears for him increased. She had stopped working at the factory but spent long hours away from home, still leaving the baby in his father's care. Bill undertook the unwonted responsibilities without question.

One afternoon, he was resting on the bed while the baby took his nap. His hands under his head, eyes staring at the ceiling, Bill was deep in thought. The door to the apartment opened softly and Helen crept in. She stood at the bedroom door looking at her husband. Slowly, he dropped his eyes to look into her face. Still more slowly, he raised himself and swung his feet to the floor. He continued to look at the exultant face, the glowing eyes. She crossed the room and threw herself into his arms.

"Darling!" she laughed, but there were tears in her eyes. "Dreams do come true!" Into his hand she put a thick envelope full of documents.

Dazedly, Bill pressed his hand over his eyes, and then wordlessly—as though the effort to come back to the present was great—he began to open the papers one by one and read them. Helen stood back in expectation, but she was unprepared for the broken, heartrending sobs that shook his frame as their meaning dawned upon him.

There were tears streaming down her face now as she told him, "It's yours, Darling—always was!"

"No, Helen—yours. Yours and mine and Johnny's—and the pony's, which will be in the pasture."

Then she told him of the long weeks of litigation and conferences; of the aid she had received from the Department of Veterans Affairs; of how the medical officer had backed her plan to fight the battle alone, fearing disappointment for the sick man; and of how, at last, all the legal snarls had been untangled and the deed for the old McElroy homestead had been handed over to the wife of the only McElroy left in the district—the last of a long and worthy line of pioneers.

"But *they* will be there," Bill worried.

"No, Darling, the community has found another farm for them. The old Stinson place—just a couple miles away I'm told, but you would know exactly where it is. You are not to worry about a single thing. As far as I know, there is nothing to worry about. I waited until everything was straightened past any chance of error before I came to you, so just relax and begin to think about what seeds we will plant in the garden."

"Timothy in the south thirty, and wheat in the west forty. We can plant green feed across the creek, like Dad used to. I wonder if there is any summer fallow." Bill's voice was dreamy and contented, and it fell like balm on Helen's ears.

Chapter Seven

The days that followed were like a wonderful dream to Bill and Helen. They drew upon Bill's re-establishment credits and Helen's meager savings to refurnish and equip the old homestead. The trips they made to the large department stores in the city were many, and to the girl who had been hemmed in for so many years by rationing and shortages, there was an element of excitement in the wealth of material to choose from. Furniture, floor coverings, paint and varnish, towels and bedding—none of it was in the luxury class, though it all seemed like it was to the home-hungry young people. Everything they chose came under the heading of comfort and good taste.

Helen had the sense of an artist, and she planned to decorate and rearrange the kitchen on the pattern of the dream bungalow of her house-hunting days. A set of good china and glassware and silver were included in their purchases.

Bill became alert and enthusiastic. There was a spring in his step. His high spirits seemed indefatigable. At last the day arrived when, their shopping complete, they were ready to move to the farm and begin the tasks of cleaning and redecorating.

This they planned to do alone, rejoicing in the opportunity afforded them of a new and favourable start together.

Helen was loving and sympathetic, following Bill's ideas as much as possible in keeping the original rural charm and old familiarity about the place. He agreed with Helen that the kitchen was the one place that should be renovated and modernized, and he enthusiastically went about to pipe water from the spring on the hillside down behind the house, making it possible to have running water at the sink. He followed the sketches she drew for him, and from them he built streamlined cupboards around the walls and painted and trimmed them to her satisfaction.

The house became a place of modern comfort and old-fashioned charm and beauty. Bill and Helen had the added satisfaction of knowing that their own hands had worked the change. The effort took the best part of a month, and Bill began to think of seeding.

The land and fences were in fairly good condition, but the machinery—along with a few old, dilapidated implements—was not. Bill set about the purchase of a tractor and other necessary equipment through the Department of Veterans Affairs and the Re-establishment Committee in the district. For the present he hoped to do the best he could by hiring and borrowing. This made a visit to Moosewell necessary for a talk with Pop Barnes of the general store. Pop shook Bill's hand heartily and welcomed him back to the community.

"A shame it was, Son—the whole business. And I have t'confess that I was one of the ones who suggested Hughes be settled on the ol' place. They needed some place bad, and there was the ol' homestead sittin' there idle, and you gone this many-a-year and not a word from you. 'He's gone and done himself well,' we all thought, or else.... Well, some of us wondered if you'd ever come back at all. And then when you did, you rushed right off again—never gave us the time to make amends.

"But that's a fine young wife you have, Bill; a fine girl with 'er head screwed on right. I told 'er you'd be back, I did. But I didn't guess then how much she'd have t'do with it. 'Always has been a McElroy in the country,' I said, and now there's you and yer son.

"Now look here, Bill, this district owes you somethin' for the shabby trick we pulled. You go home and forget about hiring anybody. I'll see you get yer crop in."

"But Pop, I wanted to get things definitely arranged today."

"Definitely arranged it is. You go home, and I'll get on the phone right away."

Three mornings later, as Bill sat in his barn—his long legs stretched out beneath the sad-eyed Jersey cow he had led home only the day before, a pail between his knees—he sang, keeping time to the sound of the milk as it slowly filled the pail. Suddenly he paused and listened to the soar and clatter of many motors and much machinery drawing nearer along the road allowance of the homestead. He jumped to his feet, hung his pail high on a nail, and turned the cow into the pasture behind the barn. Then he carried the steaming, frothy pail into the house and hollered, "Good old Pop! Come and see what is coming, Helen."

Helen left her place behind the curtain. "I thought it was an invasion by a tank regiment, Bill. Johnny is hiding behind the bed, frightened as can be."

Bill went into the bedroom and scooped the little boy up in his arms, and all three went to the gate to meet the noisy procession.

Pop Barnes was at the head of it, and he jumped down to say, "We have it all, Bill. Tell us where you want the wheat and oats. We have some barley and timothy, too. And Bill, here's a man for you t'meet. This here is Sam Hughes. He brung his outfit along and both his young sons."

Bill stepped up rather diffidently and shook hands stiffly with Sam Hughes, but soon relaxed as the tall, lean farmer shook his hand and said with hearty friendliness, "Glad to have the chance, McElroy. Glad to have the chance."

"Well, believe me, I appreciate all this, and that goes for all of you." Bill turned to the group that had gathered around. One by one, the men and boys—some friends of his childhood, many grown to man's stature since the days of his departure—stepped up and shook hands or slapped him on the back, murmuring a few words of welcome and smiling their acknowledgment to Helen and Johnny. This ceremony over, Bill climbed up beside Pop Barnes on the big Fordson tractor and rode off to the fields with the men.

Helen was still standing in the middle of the yard with a bewildered air about her. Johnny had run off to play on the grass that surrounded the house, and now two large cars rolled up to the gate and drove in.

A stout lady, whom Helen failed to recognize, opened the door of one of the cars and stepped out. She was homely, with softly-waved gray hair pulled back into a roll; a rosy, smiling face; and a soft, motherly bosom. Helen immediately thought she was one of the nicest persons she had ever met. Without appearing to be bossy at all, she took charge of the situation and began by introducing the other ladies.

"I am Mrs. Barnes," she began with herself. "This is Mrs. Jones, who lives just north-east of you here. This is Mrs. Olson, the president of the Women's Institute in our district. The ladies in this car will introduce themselves when they climb out. We have all come to help you with the garden and meals for the men. We brought all the food we will need for them, so don't you worry."

"Well, I really don't know what to say. I'm so taken by surprise," gasped Helen as she shook hands all around. "You are very welcome, and I hope we will be seeing a lot of you from time to time. I must confess, I have not taken care of the milk yet, nor washed my breakfast dishes."

The other ladies came up and introduced themselves. Mrs. Barnes, whom everyone called Mom, began to organize. "Mrs. Frey and Mrs. Brownlee and one or two others are going to put your garden in. Some of the men will have plowed and harrowed by this time. Yes, I see the outfits down there through the bushes. So you ladies, take your seeds down there and you will be able to get to work soon. Mrs. Olson and Mrs. Nelson are to make the coffee and take morning lunches out to the men in the fields. That leaves the rest of us to get the dinner ready. How will that suit you, Mrs. McElroy?"

"Just fine. Oh yes, anything you arrange will suit me. I think this is so good of you all. I don't know how I could have done it if it had been left to me to feed the men, and we had not gotten around to thinking of the garden yet."

The weather remained perfect all day and the work proceeded without a hitch. Mom Barnes was something of a wizard at keeping things rolling, and as the men came in from the fields dusty and hungry, they were fed lavishly and sent away refreshed and happy. The long table was pulled out to the full extent of its many extension leaves and Mom Barnes produced a white linen cloth from somewhere, which covered the whole length. The ladies produced boxes and jars of fruit, vegetables, pickles, homemade bread, and cakes and cookies; butter, sugar, jams, and jellies; cold chicken, a roast of pork, and roasts of other meats—in fact, every good thing to eat. Mom Barnes went out to the car and brought in her own special delicacy, a large crock of potato salad. This was turned into bowls and garnished suitably.

There was raisin pie and apple pie, lemon pie, and several pumpkin pies that were thick with luscious whipped cream. Helen made a trip to the root cellar and brought up a pitcher of rich Jersey cream, and Johnny came in with an armful of colourful wildflowers, which one of the ladies arranged in a bouquet for the centre of the table. Johnny was the man of the hour, fussed over and petted by everyone.

Bill was flushed, happy and proud of his wife and son. He carried the child out to the yard and led him around on the pinto while some of the ladies brought out cameras and snapped the happy scene.

Helen was amazed, causing her to be shy and quiet. She had never in her life seen the quality and quantity that her new neighbours seemed to take so much for granted. "Where," she wondered, "did rationing come in?" She realized, of course, that they obtained a lot of the food from their own farms, but that still left sugar, tea, and many other things for this occasion. However, of one thing she was certain: everything was given with wholehearted generosity, and she loved them for it and for their good cheer and happy ways.

She was intrigued by the gay conversation. Listening, she discovered that often what seemed a reproof was really just an affectionate wisecrack, as when Mrs. Jones called across the room in the general direction of the stove, "What, is Mrs. Nelson on the cooking team? There will be no pumpkin pie left for anyone else. My, how that woman goes for pumpkin pie!" To which Mrs. Nelson replied with a laugh and a shake of the head, "Look who is talking! Your reducing diet has not been very successful, by the look of the girl."

Mrs. Frey came up from the garden with the announcement, "I'm ravenous. Now, why wasn't I elected cook's helper? Somebody around here has pull for all the soft jobs."

"Now, you know very well you are proud of your green thumb, Mary Frey, and you would have been mad if we had not put you in the garden. Here, taste these dill pickles and sit down while I get your dinner," this from Mrs. Barnes.

Helen discovered, too, that each of the ladies was known for some special delicacy: Mrs. Barnes for her potato salad, which she could concoct with more taste and flavour than anyone else; Mrs. Nelson for her clear, tart, cranberry jelly;

Mrs. Olson for some queer kind of bread, of which she alone had the recipe, brought from the old country many years before; Mrs. Shaw had her dill pickles; Mrs. Jones, her oatmeal cookies. Helen longed to tell them of Aunt Min's crabapple jelly, and such an uprising of homesickness swept over her that she crept away to the bedroom and stood looking from the window, a tight little ball of hankie in her hand. Strange that now, when everything was going so well, she should suddenly long for home.

When Helen sat at the long table, after Pop Barnes had bowed his head and given thanks not only for the food but for the return of the "boy" in their midst, she found it hard to swallow the delicious food. A picture of Sue's face—with its paleness and its wide, dark eyes—rose before her, and she almost wished herself back home with them again. Then she caught a glimpse of the round, dimpled Johnny as he sat on Bill's knee, eating from Bill's plate, and her conscience pricked her. Yet it was not ingratitude which caused such thoughts; Helen caught a vision of the happiness possible in this friendly community and remembered other happier days.

As the cavalcade pulled out of the yard and started down the road allowance again, darkness was just beginning to fall. Bill stood in his own doorway, his arm around his wife who held their sleeping son in her arms. She leaned her head on his arm.

"Not even a dish to wash. They left a spotless house behind them." Yet that was not voicing all her thoughts—they were too deep for words just then.

Chapter Eight

As Smitty walked through the gateway carrying her grip, Helen ran to meet her.

"Smitty! Darling! We went up to the bus yesterday," she cried. "We thought you had failed us, but here you are. Look! Smitty, look! Get your eyeful. This is the best quarter section north of Edmonton—or so we believe. Feast your eyes on those hills. Behind them lies the lake. See the woods... bush, I mean. I'm learning to speak the Canadian language quickly, and I should have said, 'them *thar* hills.' Oh, Smitty! Smitty!" Helen hugged her friend in ecstasy. "We are so happy out here. Just take one look at Bill, and Johnny is getting such a tan."

Overwhelmed by all this effusion, Smitty put her grip on the ground and stood looking around. "Monarch of all you survey," she misquoted. Then quietly, deeply, "I am so glad for you Helen—so glad."

Johnny screamed for attention from the screened-in porch where he was imprisoned. Bill stood leaning against the pony he had been leading around the yard. Now he walked over to the girl and held out his hand.

"Helen was so disappointed when you were not on the bus yesterday. We are glad to see you, Smitty. What news of Carlson mansion?"

"Oh, you are well away from the city, Bill—any part of it. How I envy you. This is truly God's country, this West."

"West? What do you mean west? Why, this is north. Don't you know that? From Edmonton the North begins. Haven't you heard 'Edmonton—Gateway to the North'?"

"No, Bill! You are behind the times, old pal. It is 'Edmonton—Crossroad of the World,'" Helen chimed in.

Smitty was elated at the change in both of them. Bill was a different person, Helen a more gay and happy one. Johnny, always happy and carefree, was healthy and tanned from all his time spent out of doors. Gone was the wilted, wary look that had characterized Bill; gone, the haunting air about him. His shoulders were thrown back. His red plaid shirt open at the throat, displaying the tanned skin beneath. He wore a big hat with a wide-sweeping brim, sturdy riding boots, and denim overalls. There was an air of well-being about him that caused waves of thankfulness to rise in the heart of the ever-faithful Smitty.

Helen wore an embroidered cotton blouse with short, ruffled sleeves. A dainty white apron covered the front of her skirt. A bright red headband held back her long, copper-coloured hair. The dark shadows and tired lines were gone from her eyes, and the corners of her mouth tilted up in a spontaneous smile. Freckles adorned the small, straight nose and advertised the fact that she spent the best part of her day in the open air, hatless.

"We have the garden in, Smitty—such a huge garden," she enthused. "I know we will never eat all those vegetables, but won't it be grand to share them with Mrs. Kennedy? Even some for you too, eh?" and she laughed. "The spring wheat is showing already, and Bill says the hay will be a bumper crop."

A dark premonition struck at Smitty. "Now look, Honey," she said, "don't count your chickens before they are hatched. I was born on a farm, and I have seen frost and hail, wind and prairie fires wreak havoc, not to mention rust and insects, or drought. But... oh, pinch me, somebody; I am an old, wet blanket. This is all too, too perfect. Why, it is like something from a story. Those rolling hills. That creek. Those willows. That old log cabin. The pinto pony...." She stopped, out of breath.

Later, in the dusk of the evening as they sat on the porch, Helen entertained her friend with a detailed account of the seeding, of how the women had come along with their men and brought food and cooked it, of the gay conversations and the happy fellowship enjoyed by all.

"Don't you think they were wonderful?" she asked. "I am still slightly embarrassed when I think of all their kindness."

"Embarrassed? How silly! Why, that sort of thing is not unusual in the West. Before you have been here very long, you will have taken part in all kinds of such doings—weddings, births, funerals, sickness, fires. Any emergency will gain the same response from any group of neighbours. You see, although we live so far apart, in reality, we are very close together, very dependent on each other, because the country is so sparsely settled. It was even more so in the early days before railways and highways, before telephone and radio.

"One of the earliest memories I have was of just such an experience in our own family. On Christmas Eve, we children had taken our sled back a short way into the bush on our homestead and brought back a little beauty of a Christmas tree. With Dad's help, we set it up in the corner of the living room and dressed it with painted pine cones, strings of popped corn, and small gingerbread men that Mother had made. We hung evergreen wreathes tied with red crepe paper in the windows and decorated some of the rooms. Then we all went to bed very early that night with promises of good things in the morning. We children were never told of a make-believe Santa Claus who gave rich gifts, but only that he was the spirit of Christmas... or rather, that he was symbolic of the spirit of Christmas. We knew that when Mother bleached and dyed the homely flour sack, sewed and embroidered and knit for weeks before the great event, she was our Santa Claus. We knew that when Dad sawed and hammered and came from the workshop with the smell of paint about him, he was our Santa Claus. And we loved them the more for it.

"That night we were soon fast asleep, but Mother and Dad worked on. Dad stood on the baby's highchair to tack a garland of crepe paper to the ceiling and hang a bell on it. I remember that bell because it had hung there, in the centre of the living room, every Christmas of my life.

"Mother would hold a lamp in her hands so that Dad would have plenty of light. It was just an old-fashioned coal oil lamp, and the trailing garland caught the flame on that Christmas Eve. The flames rushed across the ceiling and caught the other decorations, and then our lovely tree—the one we children had brought from the bush—caught fire.

"Mother and Dad ran from the room, closed the door, and ran upstairs to us. We were all asleep. Soon, the house was a raging inferno. Dad broke the back-bedroom window with the metal base of the lamp, and we jumped out onto the shed roof of the kitchen—Mother in a housedress, Dad in his shirtsleeves, we children in our nightgowns.

"There was no hope of saving anything. Even Dad's money, which was hidden in an old tobacco tin in the pantry, was burnt up. Dad took us down to the barn and put us in the mangers, covering us with sweet clover hay. It was warm there, in the barn, and I can always smell the horses when I think of that fire. Mother did not cry. We were all frightened and unable to go back to sleep. We lay and listened to Mother pray—in German and in broken English. She was not asking favours of the Lord. There, on her knees on the barn floor, she cried out in thanksgiving that all the kinder were safe—safe, none hurt—and that Father was alive unscathed.

"Soon teams and trucks began to pull into our yard from every direction, as the flames reached skyward and smoke rolled over the country. Neighbours came and offered help. We were taken to the nearest home and tucked into bed, and the next day we enjoyed three different Christmases with friends who had insisted on sharing theirs with us. We were given presents at each house, and a great many big bundles were sent to us so that, in the end, we had more clothing, more bedding, and a lot more toys than we had ever before had in our lives. I had seven dolls given to me.

"A New Year's dance had been advertised to be held in the community hall. Word was sent around that the ticket money was to be given to us, and on that night it amounted to over three-hundred dollars. It was placed in a new purse and handed to my dad.

"As soon after the New Year as could possibly be arranged, teams gathered from every farm and went into the bush to log out a set of logs. These were hauled to the farm. A few days later, a log-raising was held and the walls of our new house rose in the place of the old. The rafters were laid on and the roof begun. Another group of men were laying the floor, and Dad was left with only the doors to hang and the windows to fit.

"The womenfolk supplied the food while their men worked and, furthermore, replenished my mother's cellar by giving her a shower of canned goods.

"Now, those things are not unusual, Helen, and the least about them is the happy remembrance they leave with us. The donors are happy too, because there is truth in the old saying, 'It is happier to give than to receive.'"

"Why, Smitty—how lovely! I will never forget that story."

They sat quietly there in the dusk, listening to the whir of the insects outside the screen and the sounds of the silence beyond. A soft breeze stirred the leaves, and a coyote barked far away. Happiness was no longer an elusive thing. Helen had a feeling she could put out her hand and touch the very contentment in the air around her. There was a sense deep within her that Smitty was right, this was like a tale too good to be true.

Bill stretched his long body and dug his hands deep into his pockets. Helen came back to earth and said, "Bill, you tell us something—something about your North here."

After a few moments' thought, he began. "One of my earliest memories is of a friend who used to visit the homestead when I was small and Dad and I used to live here alone. I remember Jimmy Blackcrow. He was very old and, even then, seemed ageless. He never did seem to get any older. He did not know the year of his birth. 'My tribe, once big—lots of men, warriors. Now, just me,' and he would hold up one finger.

"The strange thing about their strange friendship was that my dad and Jimmy seldom spoke. They would sit on a summer evening, just as we do now." Bill paused for a while. "Or by the big heater in the living room. And thus they would smoke, hour after hour, never speaking a word.

"I would lie on the big gray wolfskin and talk to myself in imagination. The rug was sometimes a ship at sea, sometimes a covered wagon on the prairie. I spoke aloud in my daydreams, and I might as well have been alone.

"Once in a while, one of them would get up and go to the woodbox for firewood. That, except for my own low voice, would be the only sound. Each of them seemed lost in a world of his own making and oblivious to sound.

"Occasionally someone would knock at the door and Jimmy would go help the visitors with a sick horse or cow. He was a wizard of an herbalist and a real help to the homesteaders in this way. He knew how to heal a gall or comfort a sweeney.

"He would knock his pipe out on the stove, the ashes falling into the woodbox. Then, nodding his head, he would get up and go without uttering a word. Yet after he had left, the house seemed lonely and Dad became restless. Mostly I noticed that a peculiar odour of woodsmoke went with him—I liked that smoky smell.

"One day, he told me how he got his name: 'My mother, she lie. In her arm, me—just happen. She look up and see crow in a tree. So, me Jimmy Blackcrow.'"

"Was his father's name not Jimmy Blackcrow?" asked Helen.

"No. He told me that his father's name was Jimmy Onehorse. 'After his first horse die, he never ride another horse. He walk,' Jimmy had explained."

As Helen sat enthralled by the tale of the old Indian, the shadows thickened and night fell around them. The quiet serenity of the evening came down and wrapped them about. Presently Bill lapsed into silence, and they all sat quietly, lost in their individual thoughts.

Eventually, Helen stretched and rose to her feet. "You two stay here and I will bring you a cup of tea—or shall it be coffee? ...Right! Coffee it is. First, I must look in at Johnny."

The screen door banged behind her, and she disappeared into the darkness of the house behind them. Only a few minutes lapsed and then Bill jerked his head up, a listening look on his face.

"Thought I heard Helen calling!" he exclaimed.

"I did too," Smitty declared as they both jumped to their feet.

Bill made it to the screen door first, and Smitty was close behind him as he reached the bedroom. Helen stood close to the little crib, holding the limp form of the baby in her arms. "A light!" she gasped. "Oh, get a light, Bill."

Anxiety—desperation, almost—lent haste to Bill's every movement, and soon the lamp on the bedside table was burning. Johnny lay in Helen's arms. He was blue and pinched, apparently lifeless, with eyes closed.

"There is no time to lose, Bill. I think he must have swallowed something. He was choking when I came in, and when I picked him up, he collapsed like this. Oh! What shall we do?"

"But I thought he was sleeping." Bill's tones were hushed.

"So did I. But don't stop to talk, Bill—do something! Get a doctor!"

Bill recognized the near hysteria in Helen's cracked voice, and he realized that at this moment he was the stronger of the two. He, who had been wont to lean so heavily on this girl who was his wife. Now it was he who must decide—must act.

He swung toward Smitty. "Some cool water, start bathing his face. Failing that, begin artificial respiration. I'm going to ride the horse, and I'll drive back with Dr. Carney. At best, it will take over an hour. And Smitty—watch Helen!" Their glances met and she understood his anxiety. Then he was gone.

The newly-broken pinto was full of vim after standing long hours in a stall. He needed little encouragement as, with Bill on his back, he swung through the gate at a fast lope to cover miles with dust flying. Bill was in too much turmoil to enjoy the swinging gait of the powerful animal beneath him.

He rode up to the hitching rail of Pop Barnes' General Store. With only a nod in the direction of his old friend, and with scarce a glance at the people in the store, he strode to the telephone and rang for the operator. When his call received a reply, he asked to be connected with Dr. Carney's office in the next town.

In a few minutes, he turned dejectedly to the group watching him intently. "What a break to see you folks!" he exclaimed in relief.

"Wife sick?" Pop inquired anxiously.

"No, it's Johnny—little Johnny. We don't know what is wrong but think he must have swallowed something—choked and turned blue."

Pop shook his wise old head. "Bad! That's bad!" Then, after a few moments' thought, he went on, "We'd better drive Mom out there. She's most always a help at times of sickness. I'll finish the inventory tomorrow, but thank y'all for the help. Here, Olson, you lock up the store. And Nelson, will you drive to get the mail off the midnight train if I'm not back? I'll drive Mom and Bill out there."

"Thanks, Pop," muttered Bill. "I left word for Doc to drive out as soon as he gets through tonight with Mrs. Harris. Nurse says he can't leave her yet. She is having a bad time. I hope she will be alright."

"Doc Carney hasn't lost a mother in these last seventeen years. Now, Son, you start the car up. Here's the key. I'll go in and tell Mom."

Bill left the pinto at the hitching rail, knowing well that one of the men would care for it. Pop Barnes drove fast, but the four miles seemed long. As they drove to One Mile Corner and turned in at the road allowance that led to the McElroy homestead, it struck Bill, forcibly, that the plot of ground on the corner was the community burying ground, and here already lay two McElroys in their narrow graves. His gaze was drawn to the low, unpainted fence, to the neat rows of graves now flooded with moonlight. He saw the simple crosses with a few—very few—pretentious monuments and tablets. He shivered, though the night was warm, as the car drove on quickly and lost the graves to his view.

How dear Johnny had become! "Please, God—not that, not now. We have only just begun to taste happiness."

As the car slowed at the gate, Bill jumped out and hurried to the house, where Smitty met him at the door. The light from the kerosene lamp in the living room outlined her figure and made a halo of her hair. As they went in, Bill saw her face was pale. The house was quiet. Smitty gestured with her hand toward the bedroom but did not speak. Mom Barnes went in quietly. Helen lay sleeping on top of the covers, the sleeping child in her arms.

Softly, Bill put his hand on Helen's hair. She opened her eyes. "He is alright now, Bill. At least he seems alright. Did you get the doctor?"

Bill shook his head. "No, but he is coming as soon as he can. Here is Mom Barnes."

Helen looked up at Mom. "This is nice of you, Mrs. Barnes. There is not much to be done now. We were all frightened." She rose quietly and carefully so as not to disturb Johnny.

"I must get him back into his crib," went on Helen, "but I'm afraid to wake him again." Even as she spoke, the child turned on his back, started to cough, then to choke, and again became blue and limp.

Terror spread over the faces of Helen and Bill as they stood helplessly watching, but Mom Barnes lifted the inert little figure, put him over her shoulder, and began to slap his back, gently, until the paroxysm ceased and he was able to breathe more easily. "Well, well," she said in a reassuring tone. "I ain't no doctor, but I can tell what the trouble is and what to do until the doctor gets here."

"What is it?" Helen pleaded.

"And what can we do?" Bill inquired anxiously.

"Looks like whooping cough to me. If it isn't, I'll be surprised. Now, Bill, you need a steaming kettle and some Friars' Balsam. Then you'll need a good chest rub and some other things, so you and Dad drive back to the store for them. I will write a list for you. Tell Pop to bring our portable two-burner kerosene stove for the steaming kettle. Helen, you get me a hot water bottle and a piece of woollen goods or flannel to put on his chest. We can't do much more till the men get back with the other stuff. Now stop worrying, Dear. Children get these little illnesses. Best of care and nourishing food will soon make a healthy boy like Johnny quite well again."

Helen was limp and exhausted, and it was Smitty who hustled around for the articles that Mom Barnes had asked for. Helen sat nursing the whimpering baby in her arms. Bill and Pop Barnes drove away to the store for the medication and equipment.

The old farmhouse was silent and still some hours later. Johnny was sleeping in his own little crib again, the steaming kettle out of reach on the portable kerosene stove. Mom Barnes had erected a steam tent from two pieces of flat board and a heavy tablecloth. Bill had placed a padded board underneath the mattress, according to her instructions, and this raised the small head and made breathing easier.

Helen lay sleepless in the darkened room, listening for the slightest moves of her darling. Bill slept heavily by her side. She heard the car drive up, stop while the driver got out to open the gate, and then continue up to the doorstep. Quietly, she slipped from the bed, drew on a warm bathrobe, and hurried to open the door without stopping to light a lamp.

There on the porch, silhouetted against the moonlight, stood a tall old man with a heavy slope to his shoulders. Helen could not see his face, but even if she had, she could not have recognized him. "You are Dr. Carney?" she queried.

"Yes. Mrs. McElroy?"

Helen held the door wide, and the doctor entered. "I will light the lamp," said Helen, but before she could get a match, he pulled out a huge flashlight and propped it up between some books on the living room table. By the time Helen came back with a lit lamp, he was sitting in a deep chair, his feet stretched out, an air of fatigue all about him.

Helen's conscience pricked her as she explained the events of the evening. He listened sympathetically. Hearing voices,

Bill roused and came into the room just as the doctor got up from his chair to go to the bedroom to examine the child. He confirmed Mom Barnes' diagnosis and approved her method of treatment, adding only very few suggestions.

"Mrs. Barnes..." mused the doctor. "What would this country do without the Mom and Pop Barnes in it? Now, by starting this steaming kettle treatment as early as she did, she very likely saved your boy from pneumonia. Well, Bill, all I need do now is to give him some injections of vaccine, the first starting tomorrow. And I'll leave a prescription to ease the cough. Time, as in a great many instances, is the great healer. The disease will probably run its course, but we must be careful to prevent complications if we can."

Bill did not forget to ask about Mrs. Harris, whom he remembered well. "She's fine," the doctor replied. "Another boy. That makes seven!"

Chapter Nine

The next few days were hectic, but the nights were worse, and Helen barely closed her eyes in sleep. She was constantly beside the little boy, who coughed and writhed and fought for breath. At last the serum and medication took effect, and the girl was able to get more rest. As improvement in the child's condition progressed, anxiety eased from her mind, and she suddenly realized that Smitty's vacation was drawing to an end and that, so far, she had not been able to do anything toward the entertainment and enjoyment of her guest. Instead of enjoying a holiday, Smitty had taken on the burden of housekeeping. In addition, she had been nurse's aide, guide, and counsellor. It was, therefore, with great pleasure that Helen listened to Bill as he brought the subject up one morning.

"Smitty," he said, "I hope you are not planning to pull out for the bright lights one of these days, are you?"

"Well yes, Bill. On Monday, I'm afraid. And then it will be the whir of machines for me once more. I'm not looking forward to it, but rent must be paid, and you know Mrs. Carlson of the demanding voice."

"Now look, Smitty, you can see we need you here—we do, don't we, Helen?—and I'm planning on a trip back into the foothills. You see, before I enlisted, I sold most of the stock here, but I turned Bet and Bob and Peg-legs, as well as a young sorrel, loose back in the bush. Now I'd like to go back there and round up some of those critters of mine—or their colts; there should be a few. I need at least two teams here, even with the tractor that will arrive before long—I hope. In the meantime, I can use the horses for summer fallowing, and I'd like a horse for Helen. I'm afraid Paint, the pinto, will always be too wild for her. Besides, I can't see a barnyard without a colt around."

"But Bill, how will you be able to tell your horses from others on the range, and won't they be very wild?" queried Helen.

"Won't they be bangtails and knotheads?" asked Smitty, with a knowledge of the range behind her question.

"No difficulty in telling the horses a man has raised, Honey. And the colts stick close to the mothers for years after, and the colts of a colt. And Smitty, that young sorrel of mine was no knothead, let me tell you. Bangtail he may have, though in that country the grazing runs to clean pea vine and vetch, not thistle or foxtail; the underbrush is bush.

"I am sure he has grown into a fine horse. He was two the year I turned him loose and should, by now, have outgrown his teething stage and have developed into something good. The bay was a young mare. She would be old by now if she is still alive, but it's the colts I'm thinking of. The same with the mare from the dapple team, Bet and Bob. Too old ever to be of much use again, but Bet had a couple of colts with her when I turned them loose, a short yearling and one rising two. I'm counting on those two, but I'd like to see old Bob again."

Bill was silent for a while, and Helen knew he was travelling the old-wood road again—the road that ran beside the creek and climbed the hills—as the sleigh creaked in the frosty air, or perhaps sitting on a disk as the dust of the land flew up to fill his nostrils. His land. His team.

"You want me to stay with Helen while you go?"

"Yes, Smitty, I do. I could not leave her alone, even now that Johnny is on the road to recovery. We're too far from town—no telephone, no near neighbours."

"How long will you be gone? I might be able to get another two weeks off; I could phone the factory to ask."

"No, Smitty. I want you to stay until the crop is in, and even longer. Will you stay? We—all three—want you. We need you! We can pay the going wages. Please say you'll stay. After all, Helen grew up in a large, industrial city in England—a far cry from Moosewell. She knows so little about the ways of a farm. Who better could teach her than you?" Bill's smile was pleading.

Helen and Smitty looked at each other across the table. Quickly, their faces became glowing, radiant. Their hands met in a squeeze.

"Now look, you two girls," warned Bill, "it isn't going to be all sunshine and laughter. I felt so sure that Smitty would agree to stay that I wired for five-hundred baby chicks, some

Leghorn pullets, and a few Hampshire cockerels for meat. And there is that big garden to be taken care of; the weeds are really beginning to sprout. And, of course, that son of mine comes first, and he's going to be a full-time job for some time to come. Now, what do you say?"

"I was looking over your chicken barn only yesterday, Bill, and thinking to myself, 'how I could fill it, if I lived here!' You need some young turkeys, too, and a few geese for their feathers."

"Now take it easy, young lady. I never raised a goose or a turkey in my life! However, from now on, you are the boss of the poultry department, and a goose-feather pillow does feel good. Mom Barnes might be able to tell you where to get the eggs and a few sitting hens. I'll give you some money to invest in the project. The chickens are paid for already. After breakfast, we'll see what equipment is left around the place."

"There is an old brooder stove in the shed end of the chicken barn. And I've seen a brooder house to go with it, but from the glance I got of it, it will need simply gallons of limewash and disinfectant. When do the chickens arrive?"

"Next hatch comes off Thursday-week, they tell me. That gives us nine or ten days to get ready for them, but I hope to get away before then. It is up to you if you think you can manage."

"You can leave with an easy mind," Smitty assured him. "I shall be just in my element."

"I knew that when I started planning, Smitty," Bill threw back his head with clear ringing laughter that warmed Helen's heart. How good to hear it! This Bill had come a long way from the sick man he had been.

Johnny was demanding less and less of Helen's time and, warmly dressed, he was spending the greater part of his time on the sunny porch. She found the housekeeping again becoming her own responsibility, while Smitty went around in a pair of Bill's oldest overalls—which were much too big for her, so the legs were rolled up at the bottom—and with her hair tied in a red spotted handkerchief.

As Smitty walked past the kitchen screen door, armed with brooms and brushes and a great, swishing pail, Helen picked up Johnny and followed her to see what progress she was making. Dirt and dust had vanished, and the old chicken barn shone in its sunny cleanliness. The windows were bright and clean. The air was odoriferous with disinfectant. The brooder stove was burning to dry out dampness.

"Why, Smitty!" she exclaimed. "This was really a man's job. What a transformation in the place!"

"Oh, I enjoy this kind of work. It's like being back at home again. This is a good building; the logs are thick and solid, and the moss between them is packed well. Our chickens should do well here, eh? We'll have fryers ready with the new potatoes and peas... well, maybe not the new potatoes—but soon, anyway." Smitty grew enthusiastic as she talked. "I hope they will be ready with the corn. Oh, Helen, you are going to enjoy fried chicken and corn—Southern style."

"What, in the North?" laughed Helen. "But you make me hungry. It seems that I am hungry all the time. Such a country to give one an appetite, and such a lot of good things to eat.

I'm positively fond of the Jersey. I believe she gives the best cream and butter in the country. When are you going to teach me to milk, Smitty?"

Bill was busy, too. He was putting the pinto through a few simple paces, teaching it in readiness for the job ahead. The horse was powerful, and Bill had great confidence in him. Bill borrowed a sturdy bay from Lars Olson, his old friend and neighbour.

One day, Bill climbed the ladder to the haymow hoping to find some old pack-saddles and panniers, ropes, and other equipment he would need for the trail. As he pulled himself up above the split pole ceiling of the barn, he noticed the dust that had been undisturbed for years lay thick on everything. He walked over to the pile of stuff in a far corner. Sunlight filtered in through the cracks around the door in the gable, intensifying the gloom within.

Old memories surged up within him as his hand reached out and withdrew the frame of the old Spanish cross saddle, which he had been seeking. As Bill stroked the dusty wood, it felt velvety beneath his touch. He stood there dusting it off, and a vision of Jimmy Blackcrow rose up before him.

He remembered again the old homestead kitchen as his dad had turned it into a workshop during the days of a storm, when work outdoors had been brought to a halt. The old man had toiled for days over pieces of dry birch that he had hoarded up for years, and he had been thoroughly satisfied with his handiwork. When Jimmy Blackcrow arrived, the work had been displayed with pride; but Jimmy had only shaken his head with disgust and said, "Huh. No good! Not like 'im. Hurt horse. Make saddle gall." And he had pointed to the cross that would fork above the horse's withers. "Too low," he decided.

Dad had stepped back, abashed, as Jimmy had slashed a thong and begun to unwind it. Together they had whittled and polished and wound the frame into place again. Then they had laced the rawhide panniers and blocked them over the frame until all was to their satisfaction. But here was the frame only. Bill set it down on the dusty floor and searched deeper into the pile. A gray packrat thumped her long tail and glared up at him through the dust, then she jumped away, leaving her squealing little brood in the nest behind her. Taking her place high on a rafter, she watched resentfully this man who had intruded into her domain.

He pulled a long coil of rope from beneath a pair of high-heeled boots and tested the overthrow cinch that hung on one end. The moosehorn hook came off in his hand, and he set it down beside the frame to be adjusted later. He threw a pair of heavy, roweled, rusty spurs to one side. Attached to the boots was a pair of five-point star spurs, and these he detached and laid beside the saddle. Then he continued to search for the panniers.

He pulled a tarpaulin from the heap and unfolded it. "Needs patching, but it will do," he thought and dug deeper and at last unearthed the square, box-like contraption. He lifted the panniers and held them up in the dim light, fingering the thongs that laced the seams in crisscross fashion.

Back in the corner lay the crumpled shredded mass of the old saddle blanket. As he shook it out, the family of small pack-rats was sent across the floor and a glistening, silvery object fell out. Bill stooped to pick it up and a grin spread across his face. "The blanket is done for, but here is my good ol' lighter," and he flicked in vain for a flame.

Hanging from a peg in the rafters were his leather chaps, and he reached for them and added them to the pile beside the panniers. Only the tapaderos to find now and he'd be all set to go. Somehow his stirrup would not feel right or complete without the leather coverings. He was sure they were in this heap, and he searched until he found them. Upon examination, Bill found that the lacing that rubbed the horse's hide was all eaten away from the sweat of the horses, and the rats had devoured the rest for the salt content.

Bill spent the rest of the day soaping his saddle and bridle and shoeing the front feet of the pinto with heavily caulked shoes.

Smitty took a day off from her preparations and taught Helen how to stake a grub box with yeast to start a sourdough, baking soda, sugar, flour, beans, sowbelly, coffee, honey, canned milk, meat, and—last but not least—salt for man and beast. It remained to pack Bill's kettle and frying pan, the hobbles and picket rope, his bedroll and axe, some oats for the horse, and his rifle.

Next morning found the old log house busily astir long before dawn rose over the horizon, and as Bill walked toward the barn for his horses, a chill hung in the air. The north side of the barn roof glistened with frosty crystals and the south was wet with dew. He saddled and packed the pack horse and then left him tied in front of the house while he saddled the pinto and pulled the girth lacings tight.

Helen ran from the porch and flung herself into his arms. "Do be careful, Darling! We want you back safe and sound." For the first time in weeks, fear gripped Helen's heart. Those foothills seemed such a long way off to her unaccustomed eyes.

Bill kissed her and stroked the hair back from her forehead, looking deep into her eyes. "Now look here, Honey, I was brought up in this country. I am taking no risks. Now, you go back to Smitty." He kissed her again and then swung into the saddle, a rifle flung across his shoulder.

The pinto swung round, threw up his head, and began to prance. Bill shared his eagerness and pulled the lead line of the more reluctant pack horse to start up the old-wood road. Reaching the heights of the land, he did not drop down on the other side but followed the ridge until the farm lay low behind him. Every nook and cranny, every tree and every shadow were sharply outlined in the early morning light. The smoke curled up from the chimney, straight and unwavering; there was no breeze to disturb it.

Bill looked down on the fertile acres below him, then turned his face toward the bush and began to follow a path barely discernible through the underbrush. He moved along slowly at first, planning to make only a few miles the first day, heading for a trapper's cabin on twenty-mile point that evening.

The ridge widened and flattened out into a wide plateau. Beneath him on one side, a steep incline ran down to the river flat, where the small river—little more than a creek—flowed into the lake. Tall Jack pines reached up towards the blue sky along the lake shore, but up here, on the plateau, he encountered only scrub willow and a few gnarled poplars.

The breeze freshened as he rode along, and the willow boughs slapped his face and only the wide-brimmed hat he wore saved his eyes. Upon his jacket, long fringes hung from his shoulders and sleeves, and elaborate beadwork embroidered the pockets. Little sawed-off pieces of deer horn, suitably drilled with two holes, were the buttons—sewn on with strong pieces of moosehide sinew. His trousers were heavy denim, and he wore riding boots. There was an air of utmost enjoyment about him. He was alert, drinking in the scene all around; the air of a man come home. Yes, these were his hills, this was his river, his homestead. Down yonder was his own home. This was his country.

As the sun rose, the air became warmer and the horses sweated and steamed, though he kept their pace down to a mosey, knowing he could make the twenty-mile easily by nightfall. At noon he stopped at the edge of a swamp and allowed the horses to browse on the fresh grass springing up along the edge.

He dug down deep near the roots of the willows and found enough dry twig to start a small fire. Here he boiled water for coffee and heated some beans in a frying pan. Then, slicing thick pieces of Smitty's homemade bread, he ate with the ravenous appetite of a man out-of-doors.

The horses were close by—on the edge of the swamp, eating greedily—and he laid back and watched them as they raised their heads to look around. Then he stood up and called to them, "Come, boy, come!" The pack horse looked back and began to move in his direction. The pinto followed. He fed them each a handful of oats and led them to the edge of a pool in the swamp and let them drink as much as they wanted.

Underway again, they skirted the swamp all afternoon, mosquitoes zooming thickly around them. At times, the back of Bill's moosehide coat and the flanks of the horses were black with them. The pinto half-trotted—with a jerky motion, his tail swishing constantly—looking to be rid of the swamp country.

Bill stopped long enough to unpack a roll of mosquito-netting from one of the panniers and tear off a long strip. He doubled it several times, then hung a piece across the nostrils of each horse. He was glad of this when flies began to swarm toward evening. For himself, he hung a large square of the netting from his hat, dangling it over his shoulders, but it was of little use. As he pushed through trees and brush, the boughs clapped back and tore the netting again and again. Several times he drew his handkerchief from his pocket to wipe blood from his face and neck, paying little attention to the discomfort. He was back in the life he loved.

As the sun began to drop behind the treetops, Bill's troop began to ascend, climbing steadily up from the swamp to leave it behind them. The trees grew taller and thicker and there was no longer a path discernible, but Bill rode on steadily, only occasionally stopping to blaze a tree here and there to mark his trail. The eye of a careful watcher would have noticed that the trees he blazed had been blazed before. The older mark was not healed but scarcely noticeable—wind, sun, and rain having painted the scar to the shade of the bark around it.

Bill knew where he was going, and at dusk he broke through the thick clump of trees to emerge upon a small clearing at the source of a bubbling, gurgling stream that trickled from a clear, cool spring in the hillside. The foothills rolled away to the north and to the west, and a small log cabin stood isolated on a rise of land in the clearing. Behind it, a cache rose tall on four stout logs to hold the supplies of the trapper out of reach of wolverine or coyote. The place was deserted, however, as most trappers' cabins were at that time of year.

Bill led his horses straight to the gurgling, frothing spring of icy water, and they drank deeply and satisfyingly while Bill knelt beside them and drank deeply, too. Then he bathed his mosquito-bitten face and mopped it dry with his spotted handkerchief. Next he unsaddled his horses, hobbled them, and left them to graze around the clearing. He made his way to the tiny cabin and opened the unlocked door.

When he stepped within, his head brushed the low ceiling of the sod-covered roof. In one corner stood a narrow pole bunk without mattress or blankets, but piled high with sweet-smelling pine boughs. There was a rough table close to the bunk, and a few crude shelves. The only other article of furniture was a small, rusted, airtight heater, and beside it lay a neat pile of kindling and some stove wood.

A smoked, dusty lantern hung from the ceiling. Bill reached for it and shook it. It was full, so he flashed his lighter and soon had the lantern burning to illuminate the dim interior of the room. In a few seconds a fire was roaring in the little heater, and he took his kettle to the spring for water.

After eating his evening meal, he took the lantern and climbed into the cache. There he found a wooden box with a latch on it. It held reading material, some flour, cereal, coffee, sugar, and matches in a tin box. He took only the books, as he had plentiful supplies of his own. After checking on the horses for the night, Bill read by the dim light of the lantern until his eyes were heavy with sleep.

Next morning he was up before the sun, for well he knew the long, hard day ahead of him. He carefully replaced the kindling and stove wood and put back the books where he had found them. Leaving everything safe from the small denizens of the bush and as he had found it, he latched the door and walked into the clearing to look for his horses.

He walked toward the spring, his footsteps silent on the thick carpet of moss and pine needles. As he neared the water, a beautiful sight confronted him. A herd of deer was drinking in the early morning. Yet almost immediately, they caught his scent and, without warning, were gone—as swift as the wind.

He found his horses, saddled them, and started off. The trail led ever upward and grew steeper hour by hour, until at last he knew himself to be well into the foothills. The air was crisp and clear and went to his head like wine. They had outdistanced the clouds of flies and mosquitoes. The horses were as eager as he; they knew this land of their earliest grazing.

Bill occasionally climbed down and walked along the trail, his eyes on the ground examining tracks he crossed. Again he remembered the hunting lore—taught him by Jimmy

Blackcrow in his early youth—as he searched for the water holes and timber sheds where the wild horses hid in herds.

His heart was not lonely. Though far from sight and sound of any human habitation, the place was full of memories—memories of the father long since gone, memories of the old Indian friend and companion of his childhood days. Indeed, he was so in tune with his surroundings that they completed his mood and complemented his feeling of well-being.

Chapter Ten

*H*elen walked slowly toward the house, not raising her eyes to watch the figure on horseback as it rode out of sight. Some strange premonition clouded her happiness, and she regretted this decision her husband had made—to hunt wild horses in the wilderness.

"We could have purchased two teams and a quiet saddle horse. Why could Bill not have done that? I feel his long absence is unnecessary when we have only so recently been reunited," she complained to Smitty.

"But don't you see, Helen?" Smitty pointed out, "These horses are Bill's own, or the colts of his own. He has a feeling for them. I can understand, and you will too before long. Besides, Bill is still groping, although he has come a long way. He is, in reality, trying to re-knit all the broken places in his life.

"This trip back into the foothills to reclaim his own is symbolic to him, though he is probably unaware of that. He will fish in the summer and hunt in the fall, and when haying is over and his crop is in, he will feel he has taken up where he left off. You will see, you will have a most contented man this coming winter. Helen, your part is... is to be patient and understanding."

Helen stood looking at Smitty, and her face grew hot with resentment. "I understand. Quite a philosopher, aren't you?"

Her tone was cutting, and Smitty flushed painfully. What had she said, she wondered, to have hurt Helen so much? For a time, both girls were quiet, but by noon the incident had faded into nothing and Smitty was enthusiastically counting the days until the baby chicks were to arrive.

Helen found herself facing a rather idle afternoon. She picked up little Johnny from his post-lunch nap, bundled him into some warm clothes, and wheeled him in his small wagon down to the pole-fenced garden. Then she hoed up and down the rows of tomatoes and spinach that were showing green above the ground. Soon her back ached and her legs grew stiff, but she persevered. "I can't leave everything to Smitty," she told herself. "Besides, the English have long been famous for their wonderful gardens. I must show these people that I can 'carry my end of the log,' as they say."

By four o'clock in the afternoon, she was ready to drop from very weariness. She raised her eyes and saw two figures riding slowly along the road allowance, approaching their gate.

"Goodness," she thought, "visitors! What do I look like in these slacks? And my face, red and sunburned! Thank goodness I left the house tidy."

She picked up Johnny, who was making a long chain of dandelions, and put him back into his wagon. "Drink, Mummy, drink," he cried and began to cough.

"Alright, Darling. Mummy is thirsty too, and we must go home now—like it or not."

She reached the porch just as the ladies—as the riders proved to be—closed the gate behind them. "Come right in," she called. "I have to look after the baby. I'll be with you in a minute."

Her own face hurriedly washed and hair tidied, and Johnny made presentable, they both returned to the sitting room, where the visitors were sitting by the window discussing the view.

"I thought it was you, Mrs. Olson," said Helen. "I'm glad you brought your friend along. I had to tidy Johnny and myself; we were down in the garden, hoeing. Everything is coming along nicely. We will be eating greens next week."

"Oh, you did not need to fuss for us. We're not company! We're just neighbours. This is Mrs. Shaw, who lives on the next place southwest—a few miles away. I wanted to get you two together, and as we knew your husband was leaving, we were rather worried thinking you were alone. So, we came over to see if we could help in any way."

"Well, how nice of you. I am very glad to meet you, Mrs. Shaw." Helen walked over and shook hands with the woman who had half-risen from her chair.

Mrs. Olson was a tall, gaunt, blond woman. By no stretch of the imagination could she be called good-looking. She spoke with a deep, husky voice and a Scandinavian accent. There was something so openly honest and wholesome about her that Helen liked her very much. Anyone Mrs. Olson introduced must be alright, but Helen was slightly puzzled by her companion.

Mrs. Shaw was a smaller woman, with dark hair and brown eyes and skin. She studied Helen with open curiosity, and there were sulky lines to her face.

"I was just saying to Mrs. Olson that you are the first war bride I have ever seen." She spoke as though war brides were objects of wonder. "And I thought I'd just come along to see what my neighbour was like."

"That is good of you. If all war brides from England are as well treated as I was at the time of the farm's seeding—that made such an impression on me—the English are being well repaid for any kindness they may have shown Canadians over there."

"Oh yes, the English are being repaid alright!" snapped Mrs. Shaw. "Did you ever hear the like, Mrs. Olson? Why, there're thousands of them English girls married our boys over there. Lonesome they were, that's all, and ready to be taken advantage of. That's what I say! Now look at our Nelly; twenty-five, she is, and never a date to bless herself with. All the young fellows in this district came back married!" She looked as if she was all wound up for a long outburst. Helen was painfully embarrassed and stood speechless in the middle of the room.

"Now look, Mrs. Shaw!" Mrs. Olson interrupted. "All those girls the boys married are not English. There are Irish, Scottish, Belgian, Welsh, French, and Hollanders, and I wouldn't be surprised to hear of a few German and Japanese brides eventually. Besides, if you will only stop to think, our girls married Australian and English airmen who trained in this country—and Americans, too. Then again, did your Nelly ever have a date even before the war?"

Helen spoke up quickly at this point, "Could I bring you something cool to drink? I have some apple juice, or I could make you a cup of tea?"

"Don't you start to make tea. It's too hot," Mrs. Olson replied, "but the apple juice sounds good to me." As she finished speaking, the screen door at the back slammed and Smitty stepped into the kitchen.

"I was going to tell you I have a friend staying with me, and here she is. She will be in to chat with us," and Helen excused herself and went to the kitchen.

Smitty, more used to country ways, waited only to wash the dust from her face and hands and comb her hair before going in to meet the guests. Helen quickly followed, bearing a dainty tray on which was arranged a pitcher, glasses, cheese, crackers, and a cake.

"Well, that looks good to me," Mrs. Olson enthused. Helen introduced Smitty. Mrs. Shaw had withdrawn into her shell and had very little to say for the remainder of the visit.

Conversation turned to Helen's impression of the country. "I've been very busy, and yet I get lonely—though I'm not nearly as homesick as I expected to be. Everyone is so kind, especially the Barneses and you Olsons. Sometimes I feel embarrassed accepting so much kindness," she told them.

"That is your Old Country reserve," Mrs. Olson explained. "Most Old Country people feel that way until they get used to

Western hospitality. Then they tend to outdo us. As for being lonely, I don't see how anyone can be lonely in the country when every light in every window means a name and a friend you know, where every face on the street or in the store brings to mind some association or friendship. Even the truck drivers and railway men become known to one by their first names.

"A neighbour four or ten miles away has a responsibility toward you, and you toward him. Here in the North, the doors are never locked. Every travelling salesman who beats his way between the farms gets a welcome—and a meal if he needs one. Every child knows a light means a welcome and a bed for the night if he has lost his way.

"Why, we even know each other's footsteps! When my Lars passes along the road and someone sees his footmark in the dust, they say, 'Lars Olson has been by—no one else has a foot that long.' I know that Mrs. Nelson has been around when I see the right footmark heavier than the left. Yes," went on Mrs. Olson, "we live close together here in the country. It is in the crowded city where real loneliness is known."

Smitty smiled in agreement. "I have never seen anyone fit in so quickly as Helen is doing. She is just naturally hospitable and, of course, that is one of the earmarks of the Westerner. It won't be long before she is completely Canadianized."

"I don't want you to misunderstand me," Helen said slowly and thoughtfully. "I love your Canada, your West and North. I like the foothills, though I have only seen them from a distance. And I like your prairies and lakes and wide-sweeping rivers too. The people are more wonderful than I ever expected they would be. But I, too, have my memories, and my home-land is very dear to me.

"I remember it in many different ways, but mostly, I think, I remember the bravery of the people over there—the war-wracked years when they hid in holes and dens, and death fell from the skies. Yet they emerged undaunted. I never want to forget all that, nor to forget the nights of terror—the dark-ness and the cold and hunger we suffered together. Those all combined to weld a bond that neither time nor distance—nothing—can sever. Yet I assure you, I do appreciate the kind-ness and the warm-heartedness of my present neighbours. My memories of the past will not cause me to miss the immens-ity—the grandeur—of this, your Canada."

There was a hush. It was as though a prayer had been ut-tered and each was loath to break the silence that followed.

Then, Mrs. Olson remarked casually, "Johnny is certainly looking better. I believe he is beginning to gain weight again." And for a while, the conversation centred on the child. Johnny was indeed a rosy little boy, and his spells of coughing were fewer and farther between. He climbed up on Mrs. Olson's knee and shared a cookie with her, and in doing so, he climbed right into her spacious heart.

Presently Mrs. Shaw rose and explained, "I must get home to get the milk pails ready. The men will soon be in off the summer fallow." Then turning to Helen, she held out her hand and very awkwardly, self-consciously said, "I want you to come and see us. I would like my... my Nelly to meet you—very much." She dropped her head and turned away, and Helen, moved to pity, replied instantly, "Why, of course! Smitty and I will try to get over soon."

Several mornings later, the sun streamed in at her bedroom window and wakened her as Helen lay alone in the wide bed. A cloud passed over the sun, darkening it for a few moments, and she heard a sleepy little voice saying, "Mummy, who turned out the light?" Then the side of the crib rattled, and little bare feet padded on the floor as Johnny crossed to her bed. She put out her arms and drew him close to her beneath the warm blankets.

"Mummy's boy," she murmured, and rubbed her cheek against the fair curls.

Smitty was rattling the stove lids in the kitchen and Helen knew it was long past time to get up, so she stretched luxuriously and then threw the covers back. Smitty was standing at the screen door gazing toward the south acres, where the timothy hay was planted. Helen looked over her shoulder. "What do you see out there?" she inquired lightly.

"Smoke haze," replied Smitty in a preoccupied manner.

"But nobody lives down there. Not for miles," said Helen. Just then, Johnny began to cry and cough, and Helen noticed, too, the acrid odour of wood smoke in the air. But it conveyed no meaning to her, and she lifted the baby into his highchair. Smitty had cooked the cereal, as well as a small pot of coffee for herself and tea for Helen. She scarcely spoke all through the meal and, making some excuse to leave the table early, disappeared off down the path toward the creek.

Helen, with the dishes washed and the house dusted, played with Johnny for a while on the porch and then, taking him by the hand, she followed the trail to the creek. As she passed a tall tree close to the bank, she heard a shout and looked up in surprise.

"I'm coming down," Smitty called, "wait for me!"

"Whatever is wrong with you this morning?" Helen asked, somewhat crossly.

"Haven't you noticed the smoke?" asked Smitty.

"Yes, I surely have, and Johnny has almost coughed his head off. But where is it coming from?"

"Bushfire," said Smitty shortly.

Bush meant only one thing to Helen—Bill! "Is Bill in danger?" she said, her face growing taut and white.

"No," said Smitty. "This bushfire is south, but it's getting closer. It's ourselves and the place, here, that we have to think about. Do you see that smoke billowing over there? Well, the fire is moving northeast and is spreading wide. It will cross that corner"—pointing southeast toward the hayfield—"of this quarter section. Now, Bill is up in the foothills, northwest of here,"—pointing in the opposite direction—"so get the idea of him being in danger out of your mind.

"I think the house is safe. It's on a rise of land and Bill had that firebreak plowed around it, but the barns will go, and the baby chicks will have to be moved to the root cellar behind the house. We may have to go there too. Helen, we've got lots to do! We'd better start pumping water. You shut Johnny up on the porch. We must not take a chance of his wandering away while we are busy."

Helen pumped water until her arms ached, but she uttered no word of complaint—could not, in the face of the Herculean efforts Smitty was putting forth. The pump was placed over a well at the rear of the house, and back of the house, a root cellar ran deeply into the side of the hill.

Helen soaked the heavy door of the root cellar again and again, and she poured water on the break-scorched ground all around it. Then she threw pail upon pail onto the sloping roof of the house and porch until the place was saturated. Next they soaked the ground in a wide swath around the firebreak that surrounded the house and the slope it stood upon.

This done, Smitty and Helen took tubs and carried the baby chicks from the brooder house down into the damp root cellar, keeping them closely covered with blankets and old coats. Smitty took the time to light several lanterns and put them down there too, with a can of kerosene to replenish them if need be. Then she tightly closed both doors from the outside. Helen started pumping water again while Smitty sluiced the water up onto the roof and over the walls and ground. Steam rose thick from the saturated house, and the heat was almost unbearable.

Little Johnny had cried, unnoticed, and had at last fallen asleep with his face close to the screen door of the porch. Helen stopped pumping long enough to wrap him in a warm, woollen blanket and lay him beside her at the pump.

The roar of the fire grew closer. Helen was pale and spent, and breathing was becoming increasingly difficult. At last, Smitty—feeling that they had done everything humanly possible—picked up the sleeping child and spoke through parched lips, "Come."

Helen, carrying the last pail of water, moved toward the root cellar door. The air was thick with flying sparks, and flames licked the dry grass along the edge of the firebreak.

The root cellar was constructed such that there was a heavy, double-plank door on the outside. With this closed behind them, they stood in a long, narrow passageway that was braced on each side with upright poles. Poles also formed the ceiling.

At the end of the log passage there was another door, heavy like the first, and behind this door was a high, wide room, about twelve feet square. It had been dug into the hillside. The walls were lined with shelves and root bins, and it was here that surplus garden stuff and canned goods were stored, safe from frost through the long winter months.

It was in this room that Smitty had placed the tubs of blanket-covered chicks, but not directly under the ventilator shaft. In here it was cool in contrast to the suffocating heat outside, but even here the air was smoky and acrid. Smitty took a blanket from over a tub of chicks, spread it out on the ground, and pointed to it. Helen set her pail of water down and, kneeling beside it, she drank long and thirstily from it. Then she crawled to the blanket and sat down.

Smitty placed the still-sleeping child beside Helen. But there was no rest for Smitty—not yet. Taking another blanket, she placed it on the damp floor of the large potato bin, put a lit lantern in the centre of it, and—one by one—carried the baby chicks to it. She watched them move about and come back to life. Some had died in the tubs, crushed and smothered by the huskiest amongst them. Smitty had expected this and hoped to save the majority in spite of all this unorthodox treatment.

How long Helen slept she did not know—hers was the sleep of utter exhaustion—but it seemed only minutes before Smitty, eyes blackened and face smudged and dirty, was shaking her by the shoulder.

"Wake up, Honey," she coaxed. "I hear voices and hoof beats. The fire must have passed." Then she was gone, and Helen heard the heavy door swing behind her. Smitty's footsteps passed along the passageway, the second door slammed, and Helen was alone with Johnny and the cheeping baby chicks. Helen realized that she had been hearing them through her sleep. She still felt drowsy; her brain, benumbed. She rose slowly, pulling the corner of her blanket over Johnny.

She stumbled to the first door and along the narrow passage. The air in the passage was thick, almost unbearable. She pulled the heavy door toward her and stepped out into the dark, smoke-laden air outside. She involuntarily looked toward the house. The sloping roof was thick with blackened ashes, but she and Smitty had soaked and drenched it so much that it was still wet and steamy in the heat, and not a flame blazed anywhere. The thankfulness that welled up in her heart penetrated the weary apathy, and sobs rose in her throat.

Smitty was crying too—quietly and deeply, but for a different reason. She stood looking across the firebreak toward the smoking ruins of the barns that had been grouped there. Helen remembered the days of labour Smitty had spent preparing a home for her brood. She put a hand on Smitty's shoulder and they wept together, suddenly weary beyond human endurance.

Meanwhile, Mr. Olson and Mr. Shaw—for it was they who had ridden into the yard—came out through the door of the house.

"Everything is alright in there, but it will take you a week to clean up. Lucky thing you have no animals or poultry to battle with," said Mr. Olson.

"But we have. We opened the pasture gate and let the cow go, and Smitty and I carried over five-hundred baby chicks. They are down in the root cellar."

The men looked at her in blank amazement. "Here we were thinking you'd done well to save your own hides," Olson said. "We could not get here before. We were fighting fire to save the town and elevators—did pretty good, too. Only Art's Barber Shop was burned, and even it would have been saved if the town well hadn't pumped dry."

"And the old, empty church, but we really never tried much to save that—empty and never used. We were too worried about other buildings," Mr. Shaw added.

"Is the danger passed?" Helen asked. "Is the town safe?"

"Yes, the town is safe now, and this place is safe. Safe as it can be. The fire fighters have gone to the Jones' place. It is in the direct line of the fire, though we have narrowed it down a lot. Now, as there is nothing much we can do here, we'll ride along up there."

"Stay, and I will get you something to eat," urged Helen.

"Oh no, Mrs. McElroy, we will have to hustle. We will be back later to see what we can do around here. It's too bad this had to happen when Bill was away." They swung into their saddles and rode off into the smoke.

Helen returned to the cellar to get the baby, and Smitty made her way to the house. At the back of Helen's mind loomed the thought of the desolation that would face Bill when he returned home. "But the house is left. The house is left," she repeated over and over to herself.

Chapter Eleven

Bill rode down into a steep gully. At the bottom, on the gravel bed, a mountain stream rushed madly through a gorge. It was impossible to cross here.

He travelled along the banks of the stream till it widened and shallowed out. Here, he forded it. Climbing up the other bank he passed a clump of willows, and in the shade he caught sight of the skeleton of a horse. After dismounting from the saddle, he inspected it more closely. The bones were whitened and it was impossible to tell much about the animal, except to guess its size. He stood to one side and looked closely, then bent down over the head and uttered one word aloud—"Bob."

He spoke with a definite conviction. There was the skeleton of the horse's jaw with teeth complete. Complete, that is, except for a right, upper-front tooth. Bill remembered when the tooth had been lost in a runaway when Bob was a colt.

He straightened with an air of resignation about him. This, at least, simplified his mission, narrowed down his search. He knew, now, the winter pasture where the horses had grazed, and he knew in which direction he should head from here to find the spring pasture. The valley to the east, sloping south, would be the one he sought. It remained for him to cross the ridge, and he thought he knew of a pass nearby.

He found it without much difficulty, and with it a water hole much trampled around and about by horse and game. Out of the saddle once more, he studied the tracks closely but could come to no definite conclusion because of the confusion of the jumble of marks. A few isolated ones were hardened in the dry mud, but they were of no help in his search.

However, one track he was pretty sure he recognized, and he followed the hoofprints along the pass until they thinned out and he could inspect them individually.

Yes. Here was Bet, with the off-front foot, cleft and elongated, leaving a slight dragging sign. Here, too, was the sorrel—round, definite hoofprints, with the hind feet overstepping the front by ten inches. The most definite hoofprints were large and heavy, and they were woven back and forth and through all the others, as though this horse drove the herd.

Always near the prints he recognized as Bet's were the tiny, light marks of a very new colt, and back of those were the prints of a yearling. "Just what I expected to find," he commented mentally.

He rode on down through the pass and, by late afternoon, emerged on the floor of the valley. Here the mountain slopes faced west and south. The snow was gone even at this height, and the short, green grass was springing up. The sides of the mountain, lower down, were covered by dense timber, and this proved a shed for the wild herd.

A mountain stream rumbled down the mountainside and cut deep banks into the floor of the valley. There was no sight or sound of a horse nearby, but Bill had followed the tracks and was sufficiently certain that this was his destination.

He found for himself a thick patch of spruce, and he dug out his small fireplace and started a glow with twigs and dry bark. He banked himself a couch of thick spruce and bivouacked under his tarpaulin, which he'd pitched on an angle behind it. There, he was comfortable and shielded from sun and wind. He boiled coffee, fried meat, and heated some beans. The food had the aroma and flavour found only in such a situation, and Bill ate heartily.

He unsaddled the horses, hanging the saddle and panniers high on the trees. He gave his horses grain and tied them in the shade. Then, on foot, he climbed the slope in the cool of the evening. He walked silently on the soft earth, a silence almost tangible. The sun had touched the peaks of the mountain, and a rosy glow set the shadows out in bold relief.

Bill stood and looked out across the valley, and on a narrow bench on the opposite slope, he found out what he had been seeking. There stood a group of about a dozen horses, heads bent close to the ground, grazing contentedly on the short, green grass. Bill was breathless, watching their every move. Yes, there was old Bet and the old brood mare with foal and yearling. The sorrel was there too, with a very pretty colt close to her tail, grown strong and handsome. The young dapple mare with the colt at her heels would be the yearling that had been old Bet's the year he turned her loose. Several of the horses he failed to recognize, but the proud, young stallion who paced the edge of the herd he knew as the two-year-old that was Bet's own son.

So far, his journey had not been in vain, but he knew for a fact that his task was only begun. Even as he watched, the young stallion tossed his head and sniffed the air. Then with a quick, excited movement, he circled the herd, and soon they were moving fast and out of sight. Bill noted the change in the wind and knew that his scent had wafted across the valley on the evening air. He hurried back to his camp and tethered the horses, glad they were in a different direction to the one the wild horses had taken. Bill knew well the rules of the range and that his horses would stand very little chance if the wild stallion discovered them there.

Bill retired early and rose with the sun, but the days passed with very little accomplished except that he was able to learn the daily habits of the wild herd—the trails they used, their times, and their water holes.

With this much done, he set about his task in a systematic way. Working mostly in the heat of the day, when the horses were out of sight and sound, he felled trees and lopped off branches. Using the pack horse, he skidded trees into place, spending many hours on the work. He saddle-notched the logs with his sharp axe, and set them up to form a stout corral. This was hidden in a thick stand of timber through which a game trail ran.

Two things made him certain that the horses would return through this stand of timber: on the edge of the timber, near the game trail, lay a salt lick, and the trail and the ground around the salt lick were well worn and trampled by much use.

Bushmen know a salt lick as a piece of alkaloid earth where wild herds and game lick the ground for its mineral content. The timber strip was on a narrow bench and dropped steeply to one side, down to the sides of the gorge where a mountain stream boiled madly. On the other side, the mountain rose steeply with a sheer rock surface.

Having built the corral and swung the heavy gate open, balanced to close quickly, Bill bided his time, riding the bench early morning and evening, knowing they would return with the dawn or at sundown.

So it happened. One morning, as he rode quietly into the wind, he saw them travelling along the game trail. Waiting only until they were compactly grouped, he then rode helter-skelter, shouting loudly, down the trail behind them. Fear lent wings to their feet as the startled herd flew along the trail, the stallion pounding in the rear.

Through the gate they went, stopping for nothing, right into the corral. Bill threw himself from the saddle at full gallop, swung the heavy gate into place, and pulled the bar across before they had completed the circle of the inside of the corral. None too soon, for the sorrel went flashing by, mad with fear, her colt at her heels. The others came so fast he could not recognize them, seeing only a swirl of angry, fighting horseflesh.

Old Bet alone stood still, quivering, sweat pouring down her flanks, her eyes rolling. The foal snuggled close, trying to hide beneath the mare. As the stallion passed again in his wild flight, he lunged at the corral, then tried to climb the logs. But Bill had built them strong and high, well knowing what they would have to withstand.

Satisfied that the corral would hold against every on-slaught, he went back to camp and settled down to cook his dinner. Then he rested, giving the herd lots of time to run themselves out of wind and fight. When he returned, he found them as he expected—clustered and quieter, all huddled in a far corner of the corral.

He left his saddle horse at some little distance and, un-coiling his lariat, he climbed up over the logs and jumped down into the corral. Immediately, there was a wild flurry in the far corner and the stallion came out on the run. Bill swung quickly as the front hoofs rose in the air, and the rope coiled like a long, angry snake and wrapped itself around them. With a powerful heave, Bill pulled the animal's feet from under him, and the stallion hit the ground with a thud that shook the corral.

The impact left the horse stunned and Bill leapt upon his neck, placing two fingers in the snorting nostrils and forcing the head up and off the ground. Shaking a headpiece down off his shoulder, where he had placed it in readiness, he adjusted it tightly over the stallion's great head.

Now with a great, writhing movement, Bill freed himself from his leather vest and wrapped it over the stallion's head, temporarily blinding it. Speed was his middle name as he jumped to a tall stump (still standing inside the corral) and quickly and surely wound the rope firmly around it three times. By this time the stallion was on his feet, shaking the blindfold from his eyes. As he lunged forward, Bill leapt back-ward, pulling in the slack rope—leaving only four feet of slack between the stallion's head and the stump—and was prepared to move fast in case the stallion lunged at him. Instead, the stallion threw himself backward and stood, dazed and uncertain.

Now Bill, too, was uncertain, not knowing what to expect next. Standing alert, he leaned slightly forward, ready for anything. The struggle between the horse and man continued for another fifteen minutes before the wild horse owned himself beaten. He pulled to the end of the rope, braced himself against it, and stood trembling, with all four feet wide apart.

This gave Bill the opportunity he was waiting for, and he gradually moved toward the stump. Then, with as little movement as possible, he dropped three half-hitches over the stump, took a round turn, then a firm knot.

"That will hold him," he said aloud, and relaxed against the corral fence. As this was a signal for a fresh start, the horse flung on his hind heels and began to fight again.

It was awe-inspiring to watch the powerful animal as he whirled and pulled at the restraining rope, but Bill knew he was tied securely now, and he kept out of reach of the flailing feet. He knew that having once been broken as a colt in the barnyard, the young master of the herd would settle down and be fairly easy to handle.

Bill was in his glory. This was the life for him! There was tense excitement in his every movement, yet a sure knowledge of what he was doing. To the West-born man, there was a depth of satisfaction in such close contact with nature and a natural pride in his mastery. This experience was, to Bill, the essence of his dreams and thoughts through the years of his service overseas and absence from home. To him, such an expedition was not just an adventure that called to his youth, it marked his return to his homeland, his former way of life.

Bill was drawing close to normalcy. The shadows were receding from his mind; the blank spaces narrowing down. The clean, cool air of the foothills washed through his lungs as he ate and slept in the out-of-doors. Here were his horses, back there was his land, his home, his wife, and his child. What more did a man ask of life?

The war years were as a chapter that was closed, and he felt very little inclination to go back over the pages. Yet, instinctively he knew that if he could but dare to go back through them, to read the symbols and talk of the events (talk them over and out of his system), then—and only then—would the shadows dissolve completely. The blank spaces, the un-faced horrors, would disappear forever.

If Bill had had a companion with him in the quiet evening, he may have then and there—in the silent valley, before the glow of his campfire—fought and won his battle. And yet there was healing even in the very aloneness, in the very self-sufficiency, that was forced upon him.

He had time on his hands now. For the next few days there was nothing to be done. His best weapon against the fear and fury of the wild herd was time and patience. Left alone in the corral, fenced in, most of them were feeling restriction for the first time. A few of them remembered their early years, when they had learned to follow and obey. Deprived of the leadership of the stallion, who stood stiffly at the end of the taut rope, Bill hoped to find the herd docile, easily trained, and more willing.

One morning, he took his rifle from its place in the tall tree. Slinging it across his shoulder, he mounted Paint and began to explore the lower reaches of the valley where the river widened and flowed out into wide, fertile flats. Here, the land was lightly timbered and was ideal farmland that was as yet unexploited, virgin soil. The pea vine and vetch, the wild hay, all springing up everywhere as he rode along. He knew it would be shoulder-high by mid-summer. The wildflowers bloomed in profusion, brightening the scene with blazing colour. The prickly gooseberry bushes were beginning to be— and other wild bushes were—in bloom. In a few weeks' time, the banks along the edge of the stream would be red with wild strawberries.

The stream curved and rounded a point where a ridge ran down to the end of the valley. Bill reined in the pinto and drew to a standstill as he saw—silhouetted along the edge of the ridge—a herd of deer, heads down, feeding while the early-morning dew was still on the grass. Bill faced into the wind so that his presence might not be detected. If the wind veered around and the herd caught his scent, they would be gone— swiftly, silently, absorbed into the nearby timber and skyline. Quietly, carefully, he lifted his rifle and sighted it, but after sitting there for some minutes, he lowered it again. The lust of the hunt was not upon him.

He rode down to the bank and forded the stream on a gravel bar and went up on the far bank, then rode across the flat and into the foothills as the sun climbed up over the peaks and shone down hotly on horse and rider. He was clad only in denims and a plaid shirt, and wore his wide-brimmed hat—

riding carelessly and holding the reins lightly. He sang a cowboy song in a clear, high-pitched, yodeling voice. "Oh carry me back to the lone prairie," was Bill's refrain as he rode along.

There was no one to applaud his efforts. The words were a natural expression of his heartfelt desire. The urge to sing rose from his deep contentment.

Suddenly, as he rode along, his horse shied quickly to one side and stood trembling, his head up, his nostrils quivering—a thing of terror. Bill kept his seat in the saddle by a miracle of balance and looked around to see what had caused the fright.

Ahead to one side of the trail stood a huge, brown beast erect on his hind legs, tiny eyes dilated—motionless. He was covered with coarse brown hair and stood about eight feet tall and must have weighed at least six-hundred pounds. A ferocious and dangerous animal. Bill recognized him for what he was: a large grizzly bear. Even as Bill watched, he gave a low grunt and, with a heavy shuffling gait, began to move toward horse and rider.

The horse stood transfixed, paralyzed by fear, but Bill knew that state would be only momentary, and he swung his rifle up and into place with deliberate haste. He remembered the advice his dad had given him long ago: "If you cross the path of a grizzly bear, never fool with him. He's a killer!"

As the shot cracked out, the great beast leapt into the air, then lunged forward as the horse swung around and bolted down the path in a headlong rush to be gone. Bill held the rifle close to his side and, crouching low in the saddle, gave the horse the rein while he spoke in a soft, comforting tone.

"Whoa, Paint! Whoa there, boy. Slow, boy, slow," he cautioned, and gradually the pace slackened and the pinto slowed down and finally lapsed into a jog-trot. He was lathered, and Bill headed him back toward the bank of the river and down into the valley again.

When he climbed into the corral sometime later to tackle the big sorrel mare, the stallion stood listlessly at the end of his rope. He made no sign that he noticed the man's entrance. The other horses began to move restlessly in a circle around the wall of the corral.

Bill roped the sorrel easily and hitched her to one of the corral logs. Her spirit was partially broken by the unusual confinement, and she did not put up much of a fight. Bill sat on the top log and watched her for some time, speaking reassuringly to her. Soon he climbed down and approached her quietly. The mare made one lunge away from him and stood trembling while he stroked the long nose and rubbed her shoulder. "You will make a fine saddle horse, old girl. You will do for Helen." He liked her clear, wide eyes. The colt, a nice, cleanly-built sorrel, stood near his mother.

There was one other sorrel in the bunch. He took a halter shank and started off toward old Bet. He hoped to just walk up to her and tie her up, but Bet had other ideas and she was not at all eager to give up her freedom.

Humans she knew—and seemed to remember this one— but she liked the range and the free life. She thought longingly of the timber shed in the cool of the evening, and the sparkling stream in the early morning. The dust of the well-trampled corral irked her, and she longed for the open fields.

As she saw Bill approach with the rope in his hand, she turned her head toward a corner of the corral and kept it there.

Bill, however, had lots of time and patience. With a word here and there and a few friendly slaps, he was soon able to edge in close to her and put the halter over her head. Then he led her out of her corner.

"That's that!" he exclaimed and swung his hat through the air to get the dust out of it. "Tomorrow morning we start off down the trail," he thought, for he knew that with old Bet, the stallion, and the sorrel tied up, the others would follow along.

Chapter Twelve

As Bill left the plateau and rode down over the ridge, he looked down upon his homestead in amazement.

The fire had burnt a wide swath across the southeast corner, wiped out the hayfield, crawled up into the barnyard, and devoured the old tinder-dry log buildings. The fire-break and, undoubtedly, some significant saturation efforts had saved the house, but all around it the land was smoke-blackened and scorched. Only on the slope back of the house and on the hillside to the northeast was there any sign of the advanced growth he had expected. There, the wheat waved in the sunshine and showed signs of heading.

A cold hand clutched at Bill's heart and he quickened his pace till the colts, following behind, were forced to a gallop. There was no sign of life or movement until he had almost reached the gate, where both girls ran out to meet him.

Helen was almost overcome with happiness and relief as she looked up from the place on the porch where she had been sitting—busily engaged in mending the overalls that Johnny had torn that day—to see her husband riding down the old-wood road. He was followed by a long line of horses and colts. For a moment, she sat very still, drinking in the scene. Then she jumped up and called through the screen door to Smitty.

Bill rode Paint at a jog-trot, his wide-brimmed hat pushed back on his head, showing the white of his forehead above where the tan ended. He grasped the lead rope that was attached to the halter of the stallion, and the sorrel and old Bet were tailed behind. The colts and foal followed free, sometimes stopping to eat the grass by the wayside, then running to catch up again. The pack horse was loose and jogged along at an even pace, keeping to the shady side of the trail where the trees grew tall.

When Bill reached the gate, it was already swinging wide, and Helen was waiting as he dismounted and took her into his arms. She raised her face for his kiss and Bill could see the tears roll down her cheeks. The tears were for him, as Helen thought of the disappointment that must be his.

With a dusty finger, he gently stroked the tears away. "My Johnny alright?" he asked. "I was worried when I saw no smoke from the chimney and no one about, but I suppose it is too hot for a fire. Now cheer up, Sweetheart, and tell me what you think of my horses. Was my trip worthwhile? What do you think, Smitty?"

Smitty had just closed the gate and stood with her back to them, rubbing the velvety nose of old Bet's colt. At the sound of her name, she swung around and laughingly asked, "Have you broken any to ride yet?"

"What do you think I am? A wizard? I think I did very well to get them broke to lead in such a short time."

"They are beauties, all of them, but especially this tall sorrel."

"Yes, I think so too. I think this will be my wife's saddle horse. We will see how she will break to ride."

"Now that there is no hay, what will you feed them?" worried Helen.

"The hay will grow again if we get some grain. The thing that worries me now is where to corral them. I see the fences are mostly burned down. We will tie the leaders to these trees for the present, and then I want something to eat. Got any pie?"

Helen ran into the house while Bill and Smitty unsaddled and tied the horses to the trees. Then they walked toward the house. After Bill had eaten, the girls told him, in detail, the story of the fire and their fight against it.

"Where are the chickens now?" he asked Smitty, and she told him, proudly.

"They are on the back porch. We managed to save most of them. Ransey the Jersey wandered miles away, terrified, but we found her and brought her back. The buildings are your biggest loss."

"So long as my little family is safe and well, I'm lucky," Bill assured them in all sincerity. "We needed a new barn anyhow, and there are lots of logs in the woods."

Bill wakened early the following morning with so many plans in his head and so much to do that he scarcely knew where to begin. One thing, he knew, could not be delayed, and that was fencing. There had been a heap of fence posts next to the grain field on the west slope, and he would have to ride over to the Stinson place and see if they belonged to Hughes, the late tenant. If they did, he'd have to see what sort of deal he could make for them. Then he would ride through to town and buy some wire from Pop Barnes.

Swinging into the saddle right after breakfast, he started off along a trail that led down toward the creek, crossed the creek, and he rode along till he came to a corner where a fence turned. It was a low pole fence with one strand of barbed wire along the top to keep range cattle out.

On this side of the creek, there was no sign of a fire and the crop was up and already beginning to ear. It presented a beautiful sight as it swayed in the wind, but Bill rode along, deep in thought, without noticing the picture it made.

He remembered the old Stinson place. Stinson had been an old bachelor, not much of a farmer, and his fields were usually weed-ridden. The house was little better than the trapper's cabin, as Stinson had spent the winter trapping. For the first time, the thought came to Bill that it was into this trapper's cabin that the Hughes family of many small children had moved when they had been forced to leave the McElroy homestead. He had heard in town that the family was big, and he had met the two eldest boys—about fifteen and sixteen they had seemed to be when they came to help with the seeding. Now he would have to ask another favour of the man he had caused to be evicted.

As he drew near the gate, which was a crude affair of peeled poles, several dogs of various colours and sizes ran out, yapping at his horse's heels. The horse paid little attention except to quicken its pace slightly. Bill rode right into the yard, and a figure that had been lying in the shade of the log shanty pulled himself up and came to meet him.

Still seated in the saddle, Bill leaned down and explained the situation to his neighbour. They soon came to a suitable agreement when Bill reached into his pocket and some bills changed hands. Touching his hand to his hat, he swung around and was off. Some small boys and girls came from behind the shack to watch the horse and rider out of sight.

Tying his horse to the hitching rail, Bill surveyed the town. The fire had burned through one corner, and some of the buildings there showed the scars where the flames had licked around them. The framework of the little church stood black and gaunt in the bright sunlight. By some miracle, its silent bell still hung in the open tower above its blackened skeleton.

The barber shop was blazed to the ground, but the elevators close to the railway tracks rose tall and unscarred, a fixture on the landscape. Their red-painted sides glared in the sun, and they had an air of permanency about them that belied their frame construction.

Bill stood looking at their proud height. He never remembered a time when those elevators had not been there. One of his earliest memories was that of driving up to the huge sunken scales, of having his dad lift him from the high grain box, and of watching the grain buyer write a cheque and hand it to his dad. That cheque usually meant the winter's grubstake, new schoolbooks, clothing, and shoes.

As he strode through the door of Pop Barnes' General Store, the familiar odours he remembered as a boy struck his nostrils. The smell of new denim and kerosene mixed with the smoky fragrance of moosehide moccasins, which hung by their long laces from hooks in front of the window. There were red-peaked caps for the hunter and leather mitts for the tractor driver. There was an array of shovels and tined hay forks; broad manure forks; various axes, gleaming and sharp; hooks; and screws and bolts and nails of all sizes. Collars and harnesses of every description lay on shelves beside socks and underwear, plaid shirts, and boxes containing baby dresses. There were canvas shoes and high-heeled riding boots and— the prize of the entire stock—a brand new Western saddle.

On the other side, the food was displayed, and there the aroma of coffee beans mingled with the pungency of spring onions. There were hundred-pound sacks of flour stacked on the floor, and glass sealers in cartons in preparation for the canning season. There were pails of lard and honey and syrup, sacks of oatmeal, and bags of wheat—all vied with each other for room on the crowded floor space.

Bill stood drinking it all in. Pop was busily waiting on a tall, gaunt farmer and paid no attention to the newcomer at first. This gave Bill time to study his surroundings.

Also waiting was a stooped, mahogany-coloured Indian. Long, shiny braids of black hair hung down over each shoulder. He wore a moosehide coat, and the beadwork on it ran into a riot of red, green, and blue. On his feet were moosehide moccasins. On each toe was a patch of green velvet with elaborate embroidery, done with brightly dyed porcupine quills.

By his side stood an Indian woman. She too wore braids of long black hair, held back by a band of beadwork. She wore a wide, pink skirt, blue polka-dot blouse, and a soiled apron tied about her middle. She presented an untidy, flat-footed bundle.

A chubby-faced Indian girl, about four years old, ran around the store, exploring and fingering everything within her reach. She seemed to be intrigued by a barrel of dill pickles. She put two fat little fingers into the brine and sucked them, ran back to her mother, and spoke rapidly to her in their own language. The woman shook her head and scolded. The man stood immovable, unnoticing.

Two young boys lolled against the dry goods counter discussing a dozen or so lightly-coloured slide kerchiefs that hung on a rack.

"I'm going to buy that maroon one with the bucking horse on the corner when I ship my pigs," said the taller of the two. "I want to wear it when I go to stampede in July. I hope it ain't gone before then."

"Tell Pop to write your name on it and stick it under the counter for you. That's what I'm going to do. I want that green one with the longhorn steer on it—just matches my green silk shirt that I got from the catalogue. That's one thing about Pop's store; he never has a decent fancy shirt a fellow could wear to a dance or a stampede. Just work shirts."

Bill listened to the conversation going on between Pop and the tall boy's father. "This is the best I've got in the store, Mr. Sargent. I can show you cheaper ones, but you said you wanted a good'un. Now, this here axe will set you back four and a quarter dollars."

"Why... Why..." Sargent was so peeved he stuttered as he spoke. "Why, I can show you that same axe in the catalogue for four dollars even."

"OK," Pop smiled to himself as he began to wrap the axe in brown paper. "Now you buy a four cent stamp t'mail the order, and yer envelope and paper makes a nickel. That right?"

"I s'pose."

"Then you pay a delivery charge of at least twenty cents on the axe when it's delivered, and the COD of postal note charge, right? Now yer axe's costed you four dollars, thirty-five cents so far." He finished wrapping the axe and, stooping, placed it under the counter out of sight, ignoring Sargent's attempt to pay for it.

"Hey!" The farmer demanded, "What's the idea? I did not say I wouldn't take it."

"Oh," Pop remarked with a sly look in his eye, "y'know, when you send to the catalogue for one, you have to wait ten days or so. Now, I want you t'be quite sure you want the axe... at my price."

Sargent reddened with embarrassment as he slapped the money down. Pop stood thinking for a while before he stooped and reached for the axe under the counter.

When he got around to serving Bill, he leaned over the counter in a confidential attitude. "Glad to see you, Bill. Too bad about the fire on yer place, but there were lots worse—lots worse. The Joneses lost house, barn, and crop, and with Mrs. Jones expectin' next month—mighty tough, I calls it."

"I should say! Anything being done to help?"

"Well, of course they weren't the only ones, but they were the worst off. Ya, there's this." He pointed to a tobacco can on the counter. A long slit had been cut in its top, and a piece of adhesive tape stuck below it, marked with the words "Fire Victims."

"Then, on Friday night, there's to be a big dance in the community hall at Cross Town, and everybody hereabouts'll go to that, I think. We'll get enough to tide 'em over till those who've got a bit of a crop can harvest it and those who've not can get on their feet somehow. Just startin' up like y'are, I know you've not got much, but those who have are bringin' in bedding and clothing, pillows, and towels."

"I don't know about that, I'm sure. Helen will want to share what we do have, and of course we'll go to the dance—all of us." His hand moved quietly in the direction of the can. "Well, here is the list of stuff Helen gave me to bring home. Just a few things I can carry on the back of the saddle."

"I'll have it made up in a minute. And listen, I'll drive over and get you folks on Friday night. There'll be just Mom and me in the car, far as I know. John has a date and'll ride to the dance."

Bill wondered why Pop's eyes suddenly twinkled as he said this, but did not bother to inquire further. However, what slight curiosity he had felt was satisfied when he got home and told the girls of the plan to attend the dance in Cross Town.

"Pop Barnes is going to drive us there in his car," he explained, and he was startled to see a deep blush begin at Smitty's neck and mount her face until it swept into her fair hair.

"Why, Smitty!" Helen exclaimed. "What is bothering you?"

"Well... I.... That day I went over to town, after the fire, John was in the store alone. Pop and Mom had gone on a tour of the burnt farms, and John and I began to talk about our garden, here, and I told him about the baby chicks. He told me there would probably be a dance and a supper of some kind, and he asked me if I would ride over with him."

"Do you think you can manage Paint?" grinned Bill.

"He said he would bring a saddle horse for me," Smitty said with a tilt of her head.

There had been no further discussion on the subject, but it was taken for granted that Smitty stayed. She had had her baggage collected and sent to her from the city. She was needed more than ever now. Each morning, she dressed in a pair of denim overalls and, armed with a post maul, followed Bill to the fields to work on the construction of the pasture fence.

Helen stood on the porch and watched them out of sight, a tiny spark of resentment in her heart that Smitty should be the one to accompany Bill on his rounds of work. Yet she knew that she herself would be more hindrance than help. She was so green in the ways of the farm. She knew, too, that she scarcely had the strength to swing the post maul over her shoulder, let alone pound a post deep into the earth with it. She heard the slash of an axe as Bill attacked the burnt stumps of the old posts and the echo as it rang across the fields. Slowly, she turned back into the house and walked toward the kitchen sink, which was piled high with the breakfast dishes.

Johnny ran across the floor and put his arm around her leg, but even this small exertion started a spasm of coughing, and she lifted him up and placed him over her shoulder. "Is Mummy's darling ever going to get over that old cough?" she fretted, and then to herself she said, "I should take him in to see Dr. Carney again, but I know how busy he is since the fire. Still, I will have a talk with him the first time I get the chance."

She went about her work of sweeping, dusting, and making beds; and always, the thud, thud, of the post maul came to her through the open window. The air was balmy; the sun, bright. It was hard to believe that over these same fields the fire had come roaring, sending sparks and smoke far into the sky, destroying everything before it. Rain still held off, and there were wide cracks in the parched earth that cried for moisture. There was no rustle of leaves, for the trees stood stark, black and bare.

Helen wondered at the nonchalance with which these people regarded the fire, the loss of their crops and buildings—busy, already, with plans to aid the victims. Helen thought they regarded the whole event more as an inconvenience than a misfortune. Yet deep within her, she was glad that Bill's reaction had been so slight. She had known real worry, fearing the return of the old symptoms, knowing how close to his heart is this land of his—his homestead.

Friday arrived with a hot sun scorching down on fields and roads. A hot wind blew over the foothills, and the trees in the farmyard reached blackened arms to a pitiless sky. The glare hurt Helen's eyes as she walked toward the pump at the back of the house. The hillside spring that supplied running water for the kitchen had been dried up for some time. As she pumped, the only response was the sound of sucking air. She set her pail wearily on the ground and exclaimed, "Now what is the matter?"

Smitty returned from the fields early, as she had been in the habit of doing in order to feed and water the now-sturdy young chickens. As she went over toward the pump, Helen warned her, "No water there. That has dried up now. When I think of how I used to grumble at the rain at home.... I did not know how well off we were. Of course, I was not a farmerette in those days."

"Well, sometimes we get too much rain too. One can always get too much of a good thing. But cheer up, Honey." She walked over to where Helen sat dejectedly on the bottom step of the porch, and rumpled her hair. "Bill will haul water from the creek. It will give old Bet something to do. She is getting fat and lazy, standing around. It will be some job, because we shall have to haul water for the garden, too. Some of the re-seeding is coming up well. The ground, apparently, was not burnt to any depth."

"Does it hurt the earth to be burnt?" Helen asked curiously.

"Oh, yes. Some farms are useless for years after a fire has passed. But if it has only been the surface burnt, the growth springs up fresh in a few weeks' time, and the burning seems to even do it good. There is one thing I am very sorry about, though, and that is that all the wild berries have been burnt out. We shall have to drive several miles away to pick them."

That afternoon, Smitty put Johnny in his wagon and pulled him down to the garden where she was at work. Helen slid in beside Bill on the stone boat, upon which two barrels were loaded, and they set off for water. "Not to the creek," Bill had said when told the well was dry. "The water in the creek at this time of year is too thin to plow and too thick for soup. We'll go to the lake."

"But that is such a long way off," objected Helen.

"And the doctor is a long way off if our only son takes sick from drinking impure water," answered Bill. "Next year, I hope, we will have ice stored for such an emergency as this."

The stone boat was a low sled affair without wheels, and as Helen leaned back against the barrels, the metal felt hot through her slacks and the dust came up from the horse's hoofs. The road was shady, however, for the spruce trees interlocked their branches overhead.

Old Bet dragged the stone boat up over the hill and down the other side, following the old-wood road. When the climb became steep, Bill jumped off and ran alongside. Helen held onto the barrels, and her teeth chattered as they rolled and bumped on their way. When they reached the ridge and began the descent, the barrels slid towards her at the front of the stone boat.

"Hang on there!" warned Bill. Old Bet leaned back on her haunches, holding back the weight of the stone boat as it bounced along behind her.

They turned a bend in the lane and came suddenly to the lakeshore at a place about a mile-and-a-half from the house. The panorama that lay before their eyes was breathtakingly lovely and Helen gasped with delight. "Why, the fire never touched this part of the country!" she exclaimed.

"No. It stopped at the creek back there. But it is pretty dried-out here too. Just a spark of lightning would set it all aflame. The bush is tinder dry."

"Let us hope that neither will happen. This is too lovely. I wish our garden was on the lakeshore. We could really keep it watered, couldn't we?"

"Well, we can haul water from the creek for the garden. In the meantime, we'll use this water for the house—but sparingly, Madam! That's orders, even if you do admire the scenery down here."

"Bill, look at the reflection of those hills in the water. And there is still snow on them. Why, they seem so close here!"

"They are still some good-many miles away, so don't start to walk. I warn you."

"The water is crystal clear, and the reflection of green in it makes it very lovely."

"Yes. It is fed by mountain streams and natural springs. The ice Dad and I used to cut from this lake in January was as clear as crystal. We hauled it home and stored it in the ice house, covered it with sawdust, and then when we needed it in summer months, it was perfectly preserved."

"It is strange," said Helen, "that in winter we must store for summer, and put summer supplies away for winter. I wonder what would happen to us if we did not do that."

"Well, you know, Honey, some people live only from day to day, worrying only about the present."

"I suppose so. Maybe they are better off, in the end. After all, worrying doesn't help."

Bill laughed. "Why, you are the worst worrywart I know!"

The trip back was pleasant. The barrels were now weighted down with water and there was less bouncing and rolling. Helen, too, jumped off when old Bet began the steep ascent, pulling and straining at the load behind her.

"She is a wonderful horse," Helen remarked. "Settled down to the old life as though she had never been away. Who would think that so short a time ago she was roaming the hills, footloose and fancy-free?"

When they arrived home again, Helen hurried the evening meal, thinking of the dance that night. "What will we do with Johnny?" she asked Bill.

"Why, take him along, of course! Everybody goes—every man and his child."

"But Bill, the whooping cough?"

"Oh! I never gave it a thought. Well, he is practically over it, and as it will be his bedtime anyhow, we can roll him in warm blankets and he can sleep in the car."

The fourteen miles to Cross Town seemed a long way to Helen, but no distance at all to the Barneses or to Bill. "Just the next town on the highway," they called it, and Helen found people who had ridden and driven from greater distances coming from every direction.

It was just growing dusk when they arrived, and a tall farmer was pumping up some gas lamps that he had placed on a table just inside the door. Bill recognized him as Mr. Sargent, the customer Pop had had in the store only a few days previous. He nodded his recognition, and the farmer answered with a "howdy!"

"Need some help there?" asked Bill, taking a pump and starting to work.

"Guess we can light 'em anytime now," Sargent told him.

Pop Barnes had moved up to the front of the big square hall and was talking to a group of men on the semicircular platform as they twanged their fiddles and guitars, tuning up for the evening's performance. A slim, pretty girl sat at the upright piano, striking a note, occasionally, upon request. A boy who looked to be barely thirteen years old took his place beside the drums. He looked over at the girl and asked, "Hi Sis, when do we get started?"

A man, who was an older edition of the boy, answered him, "Never mind. No more wandering around. We want you here now." A sign across the front of the platform said O'Brien's Band.

"Are they all members of one family?" Helen was curious to know.

"Almost all," Mrs. Barnes told her. "Pat O'Brien is the father. Young Pat is overseas with the Army of Occupation. There are Tim and Bob, the fiddlers, Mary at the piano, and young Jack has the drums. The fellow with the other instruments is Jake Vogel, and he is Mary's boyfriend. They are good. Pat can play any instrument.

"There's Mrs. Olson and Mrs. Nelson going into the kitchen with their cakes, and that reminds me of mine. Do you think I would wake Johnny if I opened the car door?"

"No, I don't think so. I'll come to get the box of sandwiches we made up. I am worried about the night air. Do you think he might catch cold?"

"Cold! In weather like this? Usually, no matter how hot it is during the day, we get a cool spell at night. No, I think he will be just fine."

On the way to the car, Helen met and was introduced to many of Mom's friends who happened by. The women were all laden with parcels of food and boxes of canned goods, clothing, or bedding. On reaching the car, Helen took her purse from the back seat and withdrew a small parcel from it. "I brought these, Mom; a pair of Irish linen pillow slips. Will they do?"

"Well, I have no doubt there will be a lot of pillowcases turned in tonight. I brought a pair myself. They are made from bleached flour sacks and embroidered. I'm willing to bet yours will be the only genuine Irish linen pair in the place."

"Oh, I'm glad you think they will be alright. I did not think they would be much, but they meant a lot to me, as I brought them with me from home."

They returned around the side of the hall and into the kitchen by a back entrance. The place was a bustle of confusion and chattering voices. Helen wondered how order could ever be brought about and food served to the gathering crowd. She stood back, watched for a while, and soon found order emerging from the chaos. There was a committee for the tables, another for sandwiches, and another for cakes and salads. Two ladies were in charge of beverages—tea, coffee, soft drinks, and milk. Already, large kettles were on the stove and beginning to boil. A woman was calling for help to set up the ice cream booth in the corner of the dance hall, and several men were helping with the heavy lifting.

Helen was surprised to see some of the fire victims themselves in there, busily working at their appointed tasks. There seemed so much to be done and so many to do it that she was content to stand back and watch, absorbing the happy atmosphere, getting the feel of it all, hoping that she, too, might someday be one of the bustling, busy officers.

Some of the ladies hurrying past her with arms laden would give her a smile or nod of recognition. Helen knew many of them to be ladies who had helped with the seeding, and several more Mom Barnes had introduced to her just that evening—though she could not have recalled a single name if she had tried.

Music drifted through the hall, and the sound of many feet and chattering voices broke through Helen's thoughts. She began to think of Bill and, just then, she heard him asking for Mrs. Barnes. One of the ladies said, "She has just gone out, but here is your wife."

Helen was already making her way toward the doorway. He put his arm around her waist and they danced through the doorway. The tune was unfamiliar to Helen, but pleasant and easy to follow. It had a strange rhythm and reminded Helen of an Irish fiddler. The crowd surged about them, and she saw with surprise that they were not all dancing in the same way.

Old- and middle-aged folk were on the floor doing stately old-fashioned steps to the rhythmic time, and they seemed happily unaware of the young fry who yanked and pulled and whirled each other in the ever-increasing fury of the jive. Others—like Bill and she, herself—hit a happy medium and swung into a pleasant step that brought a glow of pleasure to her face.

The months had been long since last she had allowed herself unrestrained enjoyment such as she felt tonight. In the very air about her there was a feeling of celebration. It was with a start that Helen remembered that the event was not, in reality, a celebration; that many of the couples swinging and dancing had lost their all; that others, like themselves, had suffered partial damage to crops and property; and that all were there because they wanted to express sympathy with the more unfortunate in a practical way.

This, in England, would be a charity ball. How Bill would laugh if she called it that! Over there, he had told her of the hijinks, the hoedowns, the shindigs, the platter-sessions, but never a ball. And it was not a ball, Helen realized as she looked around at the dancing figures. They were the very essence of informality. One group, only, wore formal floor-length dresses, but even in this group the male escorts were informally attired; not one tuxedo on the whole floor. This group stayed together in a clique, and Helen learned that they were the school teachers (from nearby schools) and a nurse (from the hospital in town).

Dr. Carney, however, was very much present and joined no clique. He was one of the crowd and received a warm greeting on every side. Helen thought it very likely that he had helped and befriended every family represented, at one time or another.

Some of the younger girls—teenagers—were dressed in print and gingham dresses. Helen found, to her satisfaction, that Smitty had advised her well in suggesting a plain, tailored crepe dress and a short coat. "You can wear the coat if you feel chilly, or leave it in the car," she had said.

Bill was wearing the only good suit he possessed—brown with a narrow pinstripe. He looked handsome and happy. Helen was very proud of him as they circled the big hall. She was utterly content—the stress of the fire and the worry over, Johnny's ills almost forgotten for the moment.

Suddenly, Pat O'Brien stepped to the front of the platform and, with a horn to his lips, shouted above the music, "Everybody swing. Change partners."

Bill held onto Helen and they swung around to the ever-increasing tempo of the music. Someone tapped her on the shoulder. "Change partners," a strange voice said in her ear, and she was whisked out of Bill's arms before he had time to object.

Helen found her new partner to be a tall, lanky boy with the air of a rider about him. He was slightly—very slightly—bowlegged, and he danced flat on his heels as though he were more used to high-heeled riding boots. He wore stiff new denims that were turned up three or four inches at the cuff and a tan silk shirt that had a brown pointed collar, cuffs, and pocket flaps. The pockets were also adorned with a row of tiny pearl buttons. He wore a brown silk kerchief around his neck, with the corner on one shoulder. On it, Helen could see the picture of a pretty cowgirl.

"That is a pretty girl on your shoulder," she said in an effort to make conversation.

"Yup—they don't come like that anymore. Leastways, not around here," he said with a grin. "Must be some movie star, I guess."

"Oh, I think the girls around here are very nice looking. I have seen lots of pretty girls since arriving here tonight."

"Well, I had to get me a girl from out of town. A pretty nice one, I think," he said with all the scorn of a young man for the girls who had grown up beside him.

"Oh! You did! Do I know her? What is her name?" Helen was still making conversation.

He threw back his head and revealed two rows of gleaming white teeth and laughed so heartily that Helen began to think he would stumble, but he moved along to the fast rhythm with a lithe grace. Helen found herself following an intricate, unfamiliar step with an ease which surprised her. "That's a scream," he teased. "Do you know Smitty?"

"So you are John Barnes." It was a statement rather than a question, and Helen began to laugh too. "Well, now I begin to see how much like your mother you really are."

"I would rather look like my Mom than anyone else on earth. She's the tops with me—best in the whole world."

"I should say," Helen agreed with him.

When the music stopped, Helen took the opportunity to slip out to the car to see Johnny. He was still fast asleep, cuddled in his blanket like a kitten. She returned to the hall to see

Mom Barnes sitting on a bench that ran alongside the wall, and she went on over to sit there too. John and Smitty danced past, and John turned a proud grin on them both.

"I'm so glad John has a nice girl with him tonight. So many of them would rather sit out in cars necking and petting half the night. John does not go for that sort of thing. Says it is too 'sloppy.' He enjoys the crowd and the music. We have brought him to dances with us since he was only a few months old. We would put his basket up there on the platform behind the orchestra, and he would sleep right through the noise. If he did wake, we would prop him up and give him a rattle so he could keep time with the music. When he was older, about four or five, I made him a wee cowboy suit, and he stood up there and sang for us.

"I guess Pop and I have never missed a dance since this hall was built—just after the First World War. The first dance held in it was to celebrate the first anniversary of the armistice. The last dance—the one before this—was a victory dance on VJ Day. My...." Mom Barnes heaved a great sigh.

Helen changed the subject back to where it had started. "I think all Johns are nice; at least, all the Johns I have ever known—my brother and my own little son."

"You named your son after your brother?" inquired Mom.

"Yes. You see, John was reported missing the morning Johnny was born. There could not have been any other name for him."

"Poor boy! Poor boy! Did you ever find anything out about him?"

"Yes, we did. A Dutch girl found one of my letters in his pocket. She sent us a picture of his grave. It was covered with flowers, and the girl promised to keep it that way. I shall always be grateful to Leni Moen of Helendoorn."

Helen sat in a reverie until a shadow blotted out the light for a moment. A short, stout gentleman stood bowing in front of her, and Helen rose to dance with him. His breathing was laborious. He gripped her firmly around the waist as though she might try to get away, and he gently but firmly propelled her backwards while he pumped her arm up and down. Helen wondered how much enjoyment he got from the exertions. She thought that soon she would have to scream, and she wondered what would happen if she did. It was with surprise that she heard her own voice replying to his remarks. "Yes, it has been very hot. ...Oh, surely fire won't break out again. You know, they say lightning never strikes twice in the same place," and so on in the same strain.

At last the music stopped abruptly. Helen found herself returned to the edge of the floor by her partner, and she dropped wordlessly, exhausted, into her seat next to Mom Barnes.

"That," she breathed when he had moved away, "was the longest dance I have ever endured."

"Oh no, Dear! You were not on the floor long. You must be getting tired. They will announce the after-supper dance just before midnight. You dance that with your own partner. Baskets are to be auctioned for those who are partnerless, I believe."

"Baskets?" Helen churned the remark over in her mind but could come to no satisfactory conclusion. When the music began again, she sincerely hoped she would remain unnoticed, and so she slipped quietly along the wall to the door and out to look at the baby. As he needed no attention, she stood by the car and drank in the quiet beauty of the night. From a car nearby, she heard a girl's high-pitched voice—"Oh, don't!" followed by a giggle—and she remembered the frown on an old lady's face as she had edged toward the door. "Probably thought I had some ulterior motive," she told herself, "I'd better go back."

As she stepped into the light, Dr. Carney put his hand on her shoulder. "How is the baby? Still sleeping? I watched you go out and waited for you."

"You too!" Helen smiled as they joined the dancing couples. "I have encountered a few suspicious glances already tonight. It was just beginning to dawn on me what they meant."

"Oh, it is only because people don't know you yet. They should know to look at you that you aren't the type, anyhow," he laughed.

Just then, Bill and Smitty swept past, and it seemed to Helen that they were completely rapt in each other's company. "That is twice that Bill has danced with Smitty—only once with me!" passed through her mind. Then she thought of Johnny's cough again and wished she could ask the doctor some questions, but thought better of it. This was his night off, so instead she made some cheery remark that brought a smile in response, but they had not circled the room once more before Pat O'Brien came to the front platform and raised his horn to his lips. "Doc Carney, come to the platform for a message," he called, and they began to dance in his direction. The couples on the floor moved aside to make a lane for them, and the doctor excused himself on the edge of the floor. "Probably an urgent case," he said and left Helen alone.

She stood there watching the dancers, wondering what had spoiled her mood of the early evening. Not the suspicious glances; they left her cold. Not the worry over Johnny; he was sleeping peacefully. Just then, Smitty and Bill danced into view and she knew her present mood for what it was. They danced toward her, and then all three of them walked along the wall and sat down together.

"They will soon be announcing the supper dance, and Pat says he will call some square dances afterward," Bill was telling her. Despite herself, Helen could not help but be infected by his cheerfulness.

When the music stopped again, a long table was lifted up onto the front of the platform. The table was piled high with elaborately decorated boxes of all shapes and sizes. Pat O'Brien walked over and picked up the topmost one. It was shaped like an ordinary shoebox and was covered entirely with crepe paper, and stuck on the top were two large crepe paper roses. It boasted a handle, also adorned with crepe paper roses.

"Who makes a bid on this basket?" Pat exclaimed as he held it up to view. "It is heavy—lots in it. Smells like chicken and chocolate cake. Who will say two bits? ...I'm offered four! Who will make it six?"

The bidding kept the price mounting until it stopped at two dollars. Then Pat turned over a little card and said, "Two dollars, and the gentleman gets Susie Corrigan for a partner."

A young girl in a green gingham dress walked across the hall and laughingly stood beside the young man who had staunchly outbid all the others. She pointed an accusing finger at him. "You knew, Jerry," she said. "You saw me buy some pink crepe paper the other day."

He pulled his cigarette out of his mouth and pulled a grimace. "Yeah—you and six other dames! Look at the pile of pink boxes up there." But he put his arm around her and pulled her down beside him.

The auctioneering went on until the table was empty and the partnerless bidders were paired off.

"What are two bits, Bill? 'Two bits' of what?" Helen asked.

Bill laughed long and heartily. "Just slang for twenty-five cents, Honey. In other words, two bits is a quarter of a dollar, and four bits is half a dollar, and so on. A girl who has no partner—or escort is a better word—brings a basket. A fellow who came without a girl bids for a box—or basket, as it is called. The highest bidder, of course, gets the box and the girl who brought it. At suppertime they eat the contents together. Just an old custom brought into use to raise money for some special cause—as now, to help the fire victims. It's a good idea all the way round, and the young people like it."

Helen liked it too. And she enjoyed the hearty meal, even though it was at such an unusual hour. There were fruit salads and vegetable salads, cold chicken, every kind of sandwich, cakes and cookies, jellies, ice cream, tea, coffee, milk, and soft drinks. Everyone ate heartily in spite of the fact that the ice cream stand had done a roaring business all evening. When everyone had eaten all they possibly could, there were boxes of food to be added to the boxes of clothing and blankets.

Then the trestle tables were cleared away, and some of the O'Briens walked around the floor dropping shavings of wax upon it to restore its roughened spots so that dancing feet might slide more easily.

The after-supper dance was a leisurely one—the Missouri Waltz. Helen drifted around in Bill's arms, and she knew real contentment once more. She danced her way through the night until, by the time the sun was beginning to peep over the horizon, she was so weary and footsore that she was ready to lie down on one of the benches and go to sleep.

"Bill," she told him, "nowhere else in the world do they have such long, drawn-out affairs."

"Oh yes they do, Honey. Did you never hear of the dancing dervishes in Anatolia? But they don't have such a good time, believe me. Besides, we have to wait until they give us our quilt." He spoke jokingly of a two-bit ticket they had purchased on a quilt to be raffled off.

They sat on a bench against the wall, and Helen put her head on his shoulder and watched the couples go by. They were dancing square dances now, and Pat O'Brien called out the steps. "They are very like our folk dances at home," Helen told Bill. "See how those older people enjoy them."

The younger folks enjoyed them too, and swung their partners with more vigour than gentleness. Legs went flying and the girls screamed excitedly. Now and then a cowboy whooped in a loud voice, and it all seemed part of the game.

The dance came to an end and the president of the Women's Institute, Mrs. Olson, walked up to the front of the platform and handed Pat O'Brien a square cardboard box. He called another lady from the audience and handed her a large wooden spoon. With this she stirred the rustling papers around and around. Then, a bent old gentleman was called up from the audience and, putting his wrinkled old hand down into the box, he pulled out one ticket. Pat O'Brien walked to the edge of the platform and called out the winning number.

Helen leaned sleepily on Bill's shoulder, not caring much who won the quilt, although it was a nice one. She was too tired to care. Pat called the number again, and she sat up and said, "It might be ours, Bill. Have a look." Bill lazily put his hand into his pocket, pulled out the ticket stub and looked at it, and then jumped up and shouted. Helen was so taken by surprise that she almost toppled off the bench, and then, all at once, she was not tired at all, but wide awake and excited. She was full of admiration for the beautiful hand-sewn prize.

"Why," she cried, "I've never won anything before in my life."

"Never be able to say that again, Lady," someone told her.

Mrs. Olson presented the prize, making a pretty speech to say how glad she was to be presenting it to the only war bride present. Helen voiced her thanks and told of her admiration and surprise.

When they were safely home again, she turned to Smitty and asked, "Should I have given the quilt to the fire victims?"

"No, not at all, Helen. The ladies were sincere when they said how glad they were that you won it. Besides, there are so many fire victims that it would be hard to decide which family should get it; it might, in the end, cause hard feelings. No—I think you did quite right to keep it."

Chapter Thirteen

The days passed hot and cloudless, bringing no relief to the parched crops. Bill continued to haul water for the household from the lake. He was succeeding very well with the job of breaking in the young horses and now had a fairly workable team of sorrels. This meant that he could often drive into town and take Helen and the baby with him and still haul back supplies. He had been able to buy a second-hand combine and tractor and was looking forward to the time when harvesting would begin.

"But we need rain, Helen. How we need rain!" he told her as they walked around the field one night, inspecting the growth. "See that wheat turning yellow and dying out before it is properly headed? That shrivels the grain, brings down the grade. This stand will now do well to make fifteen or twenty bushels to the acre. I had hoped for at least twenty because it had such a good start."

Bill stood looking out across the fields, thinking deeply. A blue, smoky haze hung in the air as though bushfires were burning far away. Helen thought of what she had said to the queer old man who had been her dancing partner—"Lightning never strikes in the same place."

They completed the circle of the wheat field, looked out along the green-feed, and walked towards the garden patch. It was surprisingly green and lush, except in the rows of straw-coloured corn stalks.

The reseeding had been successful, and Helen felt a pride in this corner of the farm. Day after day she had worked beside Smitty—or alone—hoeing up and down the long rows, carrying water in pails from the barrels on the stone boat to keep the soil moist and the plants green. It had been worth all the effort when Helen looked at the rows of tomato vines, heavy with green, unripened fruit, and when she saw the pumpkin and marrow vines nurturing their huge offspring. As she stooped and pulled a golden carrot from the brown earth, she thought she understood a little of the hunger and longing in Bill for the land—his own land.

Yet Bill was worried—upset. She knew that now. More so than when he had first viewed the desolation wrought by the fire. The new timothy hay had sprung up knee-high and the grass was growing short and green on the charred ground. Even a few of the trees had the courage to send out a few hopeful green feelers. In the underbrush, the young poplars and willows were springing up, thick and undaunted. Soon the charred old ones, their sap cut off by the intense heat of the fire, would drop to be hauled away, or they would lie there, a home for the ant and the wild squirrel, while the young trees would grow tall, reach to the sky, and replace the dead ones.

Arriving home, Bill stood for a long time looking at the laden sky, the smoke haze, before turning in. It seemed to Helen that they had scarcely closed their eyes before a loud pounding at the door wakened them. Bill sprang to the floor, and Helen was quick to wrap a kimono around herself and follow him through the living room. It was pitch dark outside, and the lamp that Bill had lit and was holding up slashed the darkness, revealing the figure of a young boy standing on the porch, twisting an old peanut-straw hat in his hands.

"Mr. McElroy," the boy said in obvious agitation, "Ma's took sick, and Jimmy and Pa went to Cross Town this afternoon to see about shippin' some pigs. I will go get Dr. Carney if you and Mrs. McElroy will go on over to Ma. She can't be left alone with only the young'uns there. Ruth is only eleven, and Connie nine. They won't be much use."

"You go on, Son. We will leave right away." Bill was abrupt and definite.

As Helen dressed hurriedly, she heard the clop, clop of the horse's hoofs going off into the night. Bill stopped only long enough to pull trousers over his pajamas, put on a sweater and slippers, and while he was harnessing the young team, Helen pulled Johnny's crib into Smitty's room across the kitchen. Then she made up a bundle of sheets and towels, a hot water bottle, some disinfectant, scissors, and tape. She did not know what to expect.

She was standing on the steps with her bundle in her arms waiting for Bill when he drove up. The horses were acting up and Bill shouted, "Jump in, quick. I can hardly hold them."

Helen jumped, though her heart was in her mouth, and the horses were off like a shot. Bill stood up in front of the rig and held onto the lines with all his might. Helen clung to the seat with one hand and gripped her bundle with the other, almost petrified with fear. There was something frightful in this wild slashing through the night, in darkness that hid the road to an unknown house and unknown people—who, nevertheless, needed her help.

The steep climb up the hill had tired the horses and presently they slowed down; Bill appeared to have better control of them. He spoke reassuringly to Helen, "I was afraid a line might snap, but we will be alright now. Are you warm enough?"

"Warm! I'm perspiring," she laughed shakily. She heard the rattle and the hollow sound of a bridge beneath them.

"We'll soon be there. It is just across the creek here." And there before them, a gate swung open and a small girl stood vigil in the darkness beside it.

As Bill was tying the team, Helen climbed out and walked over to the child.

"I could not listen to Ma crying. She's awful bad. I came out here to wait for someone," she said.

Helen put an arm around the thin shoulders of the trembling child. "Let's go inside now and get warm," she coaxed, and together they went toward the house.

As the door swung open, Helen saw a dim light burning behind a curtain, which hung around a bed in one corner. The air was fetid, as though no window or door had been open at this time of year. A low moan came from behind the curtain, and there was also the sound of the breathing of sleeping children. A child turned in his bed somewhere in the darkness and shouted, "Give that to me! Give it to me!" giving expression to his dreams. A pain-wracked voice came from behind the curtain. "Go to sleep, Sonny," it said.

Helen parted the curtain and stepped behind. "Mrs. Hughes," she said, "We've come to help you if we can."

"Oh! God bless you. God bless you. My man is away!" Here, pain caught the woman and swept her voice away. Her hand groped for the rusty iron bedstead above, and she grasped the rail tightly.

"Oh! My God! My God!" she screamed hoarsely.

A small, miserable figure sat at the foot of the bed. Helen would have scarcely noticed her but for a sob which broke from the crouching girl. Helen bent over and patted her, saying, "Sweetheart, you must go back to bed. I'm here to take care of Mummy now."

"Oh, I can't. I can't listen to Ma crying like that, and I can't go out like Ruthie done, either."

Just then, Bill stepped through the door and Helen took each of the two little girls by the hand and led them out to him. "Find their bed, Bill. Get their blankets and take them both, and make them a bed in our rig. I shall need the bundle I brought—right away, too." Then she slipped back behind the curtain again.

When she looked down at the writhing figure on the bed, a sudden revulsion took possession of her—a nausea and fear of the task ahead of her. It rose up around her and she almost blacked out beneath it, but she knew what had to be done and gathered her courage to do it.

Memory stood her in good stead. She remembered every movement of the two old grannies who had delivered a war baby in the narrow confines of a public air raid shelter, while bombs crashed nearby and the screams of the young mother were drowned out by the crash of failing masonry. She bent over the moaning woman, turned back the covers, and slid her own clean sheet in over the ragged quilt that the woman lay upon. Then, leaving her briefly, she went in search of a stove on which to heat water. In a moment she was back, her cool hands soothing and comforting when needed. The hours dragged on, and Helen found herself straining to hear the sounds of a horse's hoofs or the purr of a motor bringing the doctor.

In the last stages, Helen was kept busy as her patient became a screaming, frenzied body of pain. Other children had wakened in the house and they kept Bill busy on the other side of the curtain until, at last, she had to call him to leave them and come to her to help.

Between Helen and Bill, they took the tiny bundle from the exhausted mother and laid it on the bed. Then Helen mouthed hurried instructions to Bill on the care of the baby whilst she, herself, tended the desperate woman. To her surprise, and Bill's, the poor woman had more pain to come. Twenty minutes later, another little bundle was laid alongside the first. This one was too quiet, making no effort to breathe, and Helen set to work—slapping it, dipping it in warm water, and calling to Bill for cold. At last she put her own mouth down over the tiny, silent one and breathed into it. With a gasp, a cry, the inert little form came to life.

The mother moaned on the bed. The twins screamed at her feet and children whimpered on the other side of the curtain, but Helen was unaware of the noise and confusion. A feeling of relief surged within her as she looked at those two tiny babies, so evidently alive and kicking. She bundled each in a torn half of her own good sheet and put them down on a blanket that Bill had placed in the bottom of a washtub.

Turning to the woman, who lay white and exhausted, Helen realized how much she had endured. Now a sudden shivering shaking took possession of her, and the bed rattled beneath her. Helen recognized the danger signal.

"Bill," she cried, "have they any brandy in the house? Look Bill! Hunt all over the place for something while I fill the hot water bottle again."

Quickly, she gathered all the blankets she could find and wrapped the woman up. Bill brought a glass of colourless liquid. "Moonshine, I think," he said, "but all I could find."

Helen raised the patient's head and let a few drops of the fiery liquid roll down her throat. "If only she'll sleep," she prayed, and she shuddered involuntarily.

Together they raised the end of the bed and put wooden blocks under it. Then they pulled the blankets up tight around her. In a few minutes, their efforts were rewarded by a cessation of the violent trembling, and the tired woman fell asleep.

They hushed the children and warmed milk for them, and it was with intense thankfulness that at last they heard Dr. Carney's car turn in at the gate and the doctor's footsteps coming up to the door. The boy leapt through the door, and Dr. Carney followed hurriedly behind.

Helen said, "Twins have arrived and all are sleeping, but she needs your help, Doctor, I am sure."

When the doctor came back from behind the curtain, he smiled and said, "Sleep is the answer in this case. Best medicine she can have just now, but if you will bring those babies to me, I will tend to their eyes."

"I have not even had time to bathe them yet and I haven't any oil; have you some, Doctor?"

"Yes! Yes, I have. You have done very well, Mrs. McElroy."

For the first time, Helen was able to relax and look around the shabby cabin. In one corner there were two sets of bunks nailed to the walls. On the north and west walls were bunks three deep and at right angles to each other. One set was longer than the other, this being for the older children and the shorter set for the younger. A bottom bunk held a double load and two small tow-headed boys slept together, their arms and legs entwined, covered only by an old, knit sweater. The children in the other bunks were covered by an assortment of coats and jackets, Helen and Bill having commandeered all the blankets for the mother's bed.

"These are the people who were in our place?" Helen asked the doctor, though she thought she knew the answer.

"Yes. You see, the place had been taken over by the community and the welfare authorities placed them there. Then they placed them here when you reclaimed your homestead, as this was the only available place in the community. He was in the army for a few months, never overseas, and then discharged. The mother has had a lot of illness, but as for the man himself, he is a hopeless, helpless type of individual. The boy Rod, who came for me, has all his wits about him and thinks a lot of his mother. Feels it, too—the way they live."

Helen glanced at the boy. He was stoking wood into the rusty iron stove in an attempt to keep the drafty cabin warm. Helen could see stars shining between the log walls in places. She shuddered to think what the place would be like in winter and was thankful that tonight the air was warm. Finished with the fire, Rod moved over to stand beside the doctor and watched as he worked with the twins.

"Mother OK?" he asked the doctor anxiously, in a gruff voice.

"Yes, Son, I think she will be fine," the doctor answered with more assurance than he felt.

"These kids will make a lot more work for her," Rod went on, almost resentfully.

"Oh, she won't mind. Mothers don't, somehow," Helen told him.

"How is your garden?" she asked him—to make conversation and change his thoughts.

"Haven't got any—too dry, too many weeds."

Helen thought of her garden—burnt out, reseeded—and of the water they had hauled to keep it growing and green.

"You come over tomorrow. I will give you some tomatoes to ripen in the window for Mother, and some corn and green stuff for the kiddies and you, eh?"

"I will have to stay here with Mother and the kids, but I'll send Ruthie and Connie—and thanks a lot."

"Will you take Mrs. Hughes to hospital?" Helen asked Dr. Carney.

"Yes, I think so, if she can be moved when she wakes."

It was daylight when Helen and Bill drove home. The air was heavy, the haze intensified. Smitty was feeding Johnny his breakfast when they arrived, her eyes heavy with anxiety.

"I could not imagine where you had gone when I wakened to find Johnny in my room," she said. Then I found the sorrel team gone and I really began to worry, because I know how they acted up when Bill hitched them to the cultivator. They are too full of oats, I think."

"I too," laughed Helen. "We almost had a runaway in the pitch darkness last night," and she went on to tell all about Mrs. Hughes and the babies.

"We could cook a jar of beans and make a big pudding to send back with the little girls," Smitty suggested.

"We will certainly have to do something like that," Helen agreed. "Dr. Carney is taking the mother and babies to hospital in Cross Town this morning, I think."

Bill had very little to say and stood on the porch looking out over the fields. A frown creased his forehead, and Helen felt an air of tense worry about him again. "How about a rest for a while," she coaxed.

"No. Give me some coffee. Just coffee," he answered shortly.

When he had left the table and was walking toward the temporary lean-to shed that he'd built near the corral for the horses, Helen turned to Smitty and asked, "Do you think Bill is worrying about another fire?" with something like fear in her voice.

"No, Honey, it is hail he is thinking about. This is hail weather, and you know Bill did not insure his crop."

"I never heard of anyone insuring crops against hail."

"Well, they do in hail districts, but apparently there has been very little hail around here, and none of the crops are insured. John Barnes says he can remember hail only once before."

After dinner, Smitty went around the outside of the house to secure what she could against the potential storm. Helen was washing the dinner dishes when the first clap of thunder rolled over the house. It broke so close that it left her trembling.

Johnny had been sitting under the table contentedly piling blocks one upon another. With the first clap of thunder, he caught up a tailless rag puppy and held it tight to him; and with the second, he slowly climbed to his feet and moved toward his mother.

"Gun shoots, Mummy, gun shoots?" he asked her.

"No, Sweetheart. No guns here." She lifted him up and walked to the screen door just as the first hailstones hit the roof and bounced off—slowly at first, one at a time, but there was a roaring far away and coming closer. Smitty ran across the yard holding a pan over her head, and the hailstones began to fall thick and fast. They pelted the shake roof and bounced off the chimney, rolling to the ground in heaps like fine white pebbles.

"It looks like an old-fashioned tapioca, only much bigger," Helen remarked.

"The windows on the side of the house are safe, but the back ones might break as the hail is driving that way. We used to pad the windows with mattresses and blankets at home. Let's try that."

Helen ran for the crib mattress and held it against the long window above the sink. She could feel the steady vibration of the hailstones as they pelted against it. Johnny held tight to her leg, chewing the hem of her dress in his nervousness, and she spoke to him. "Funny noise, Johnny," she said and smiled encouragingly.

"This back bedroom window is broken already, but the side ones will be alright, I think," called Smitty. She added, "Here comes Bill on the run."

A few seconds later the door burst open and Bill dashed in, head down, clothes soaking. "I knew it was coming," he said. As he walked through to the kitchen, little rivulets of water ran down his legs and onto the floor. The sun had been replaced by a twilight darkness, and there was a chill in the air.

Helen had allowed the fire to die after dinner, and she now left the mattress, propped against the window, to reach down behind the stove for kindling. There were only some sticks of coarse wood, and Bill took his pocket knife to shave off some fine curls to start the fire. As Helen lifted the stove lid, thunder clapped directly overhead and she felt a tremor along her arm.

"That was close," Bill said.

"And how close!" Helen agreed as she stood looking at her tingling fingers.

Smitty was still busy blocking the broken window so that the hail could not fall into the bedroom. The fire began to blaze and she came to stand near the heat, gratefully.

"It's the first time in days that I have really appreciated a fire," she said thoughtfully.

"Oh, I was glad of one in the drafty cabin last night," Helen told her. "Those poor children! I hope their dad is back and the mother safe in hospital."

"They are out of luck for tomatoes and corn now, Honey," Bill warned her.

"I suppose so." But she was totally unprepared for the scene of destruction that faced her when they walked down to the garden and fields after the storm had cleared, leaving a gray overcast.

On first stepping off the porch, she was elated at the clean fragrance that filled the air. The drought was at an end, the heat wave broken. But on reaching the gate, she stood by it, watching the little muddy streams of water running down the rows. The vines were plowed into the ground, tomatoes smashed, pumpkins torn from the stalk. The beans were blackened and broken, turnip and carrot tops bent flat on the ground. Only the cabbage heads stood proud and unhurt.

"It looks as though it had been harrowed," she said sadly.

"Thank goodness all the chicks were inside feeding, or they would be minus their heads," was Smitty's comment.

Bill looked beyond the garden to the wheat field that skirted it. The wheat lay in swaths close to the ground, all the grain threshed from the heads. There was no remedy for that state of affairs, and Bill knew it. Only that morning, when he had made his rounds of inspection after breakfast, the wheat had stood ripe, ready to be combined, and he had decided to try to muster a crew. Now he said, "Guess I won't be using that combine this year after all," and he turned back to the house.

The girls followed wordlessly.

Chapter Fourteen

The days that followed were difficult ones. Smitty spent the greater part of her time in the slab shed that had become the chicken house. Well she knew, with the keen understanding she possessed, that these young people were best left to battle their disappointment alone.

Bill said very little to anyone and Helen knew better than to offer him sympathy. After all, this was the life of a farmer. The life he had chosen. She knew he would solve their problem somehow, if given time, and she was willing to leave him to his own thoughts.

She was thankful, too, that the dry, hot days were at an end, that the dust had settled on the trails and roadways. She heard from Bill that every farmer west of the highway had been hailed out and knew that they were not alone in their loss. With the abundance they enjoyed, poverty was not hard to bear, she mused. It was true that they had an abundance of cream and milk and chickens. To the English girl, this seemed something close to abundance, and she found it very hard to worry about the fact that cash was short.

The Shaws, southwest of their place, had lost all their grain except one field of green feed. The Joneses, on the northeast side, had been completely burnt out. John Barnes, who farmed the quarter-section for his dad, had been hailed out. Indeed, out of all who had been hailed out or had lost everything by fire, and those who had missed both fire and hail, the Olsons alone had a fair crop still standing.

Helen began to wonder if—after all—they had been wise to move from the city. Time is a great eraser, and she had almost forgotten the inconvenience of the tiny basement suite. A great loneliness swept over her for Ma Kelly and Mrs. Kennedy. She went into her bedroom and dug up every letter she had received from Dad and Sue and Aunt Min. She unearthed the old album of family snapshots, and great tears dropped as she pored over them in a wave of homesickness such as she had never felt in all the busy days before the storm.

At night she lay in bed and remembered the factory and the steadily increasing paycheque she had drawn every week. To her unfamiliar eyes, farming seemed to be more of a risk than anything else. She relived, again, the terror of the fire and the swift calamity of the hail.

Bill could and should have seen the growing aversion in her attitude, but he was so fully occupied in trying to find ways and means to make ends meet that he paid less attention than usual to the girl who was so far from her father's home and her friends. Helen noticed his apparent neglect of her and began to apply a different reason for his actions.

So it is that the wholesome fabric of our lives will sometimes crumple around us while we are unaware.

One evening, Helen was sitting on the top step of the porch—chin in hand, an absent look in her eye. Smitty came out to her from the kitchen, where she had been putting away the supper things. Johnny was already bathed and asleep.

"I have a suggestion to make," she announced.

Helen looked up with a start. "Anything! Anything is alright with me. I am so tired of doing just nothing all day long."

"Let's take the sorrel team tomorrow morning and go up over the ridge and along the lakeshore to hunt for wild berries where the fire and hail did not hit," she said. "Bill could take his fishing tackle and fish in the lake while we pick berries, if we find any."

"Always thinking of Bill!" flashed through Helen's mind as she answered aloud, "OK." The tone was less enthusiastic than it might have been.

The plan suited Bill when Smitty put it up to him, and he set about hunting for his wallet of hooks and flies, of which he had a good collection. He reached above the door of the living room and took down a long telescope fishing rod, which shared honours with a rifle that hung on the antlers of a huge deer head. He attached a reel to the rod and went in search of an old creel he had seen hanging on the back porch.

Helen and Smitty packed a lunch box with fried chicken, baking powder biscuits, glass jars of cold milk, homemade gingersnaps, and a kettle to boil their coffee. Helen sat beside Bill on the front seat behind the horses, Johnny on her knee. Smitty lolled in the back of the rig where there was no seat, her back propped up against the lunch boxes. They travelled from about eight o'clock in the morning—up over the ridge, down the other side, across the stream, and along the lakeshore. Flies whizzed about them, and Helen kept brushing them off the baby with her hand.

Bill turned his head, often toward Smitty, to point out landmarks and characteristics, saying again and again, "You have nothing like that out on the prairies."

"Who cares about the prairies?" thought Helen. But in spite of herself, she felt better to be about and doing something. "I was really getting in a rut. I had even forgotten about those poor children. Why, what is the matter with me? A hail storm is not nearly so bad as a buzz bomb! Even the bush-fire. Why, not one person was burnt in it!" She chewed these thoughts over as they rode along.

Before noon, they camped on the shore of a little inlet. "Green Bay, this is called," Bill told them. "You can see the reason for its name. The spruce trees along the shore are re-flected in the clear water."

"It is beau-ti-ful!" said Helen with emphasis, and she meant it with all her heart.

Smitty had disappeared into the underbrush and now shouted back, "Cranberries! Chokecherries galore!"

"There should be some huckleberries back farther, against that little hill—used to be, years ago," Bill told them.

The fire started and the coffee boiling, Helen suddenly realized that she was famished. The coffee had that smoky, fra-grant tang it has when boiled outdoors. The cold chicken was delicious and the biscuits appetizing. Some of the discontent, the fretfulness, began to slip from her shoulders. But she could not help thinking, "It had to be Smitty who found the berries, just as she thought up this picnic. It is Smitty this and Smitty that. I'm beginning to look like a dumb-cluck beside her, and Bill really admires her. Well, he used to think I was alright too... in my own setting. I can understand that I am at a disadvantage here, but surely I have not changed so very much."

Luncheon was over and Helen would have liked to lie back on the green carpet of fragrant pine needles and doze awhile, but the others were already equipped with pails, slung on belts to leave both hands free for picking, so Helen prepared to be off, too.

"We will wait for you at the first clump of berries back here," Bill called as he and Smitty parted the bushes and disappeared.

Helen rolled Johnny in a blanket, put an old cushion under his head, gave him a gingersnap, then sat down beside him. He was asleep almost instantly and she waited only long enough to be quite sure, then she went through the bushes after the other two. As she approached from around a thick tree, she thought she saw Smitty step back suddenly, then move around to the opposite side of the bush she and Bill were picking, but Helen said nothing. Choosing a low bush, she began to strip the glossy berries into her pail.

Bill turned his head and said, "You there, Honey? Did you get your son to sleep?"

"Yes. He is fast asleep." As Helen replied, she thought scornfully, "Everybody calls everybody else 'Honey' around here. It doesn't mean a thing!"

She applied herself to the task of picking intently, and she listened to Johnny stir and whimper in his sleep several times before he grew too restless. Then she ran back through the bushes to the foot of the tree where he slept. She unwrapped him from his blanket, bathed his mosquito-bitten little face with cool water from the lake, tied on his shoes, and led him back into the bush.

She had filled her pail once and emptied it into the box left in the rig for that purpose. Now she began again, and the berries rattled down into the pail, bouncing on the bottom with a rhythmic sound. Her fingertips were stained, as were her lips and teeth, from the berries she had tasted. Johnny sat down at her feet and began to build little mountains with pine cones. She could hear Bill and Smitty further up the hillside, where they had gone to hunt for huckleberries.

Soon Bill came back, and taking Johnny by the hands, he swung him up onto his back. "Come on, Helen, dump those chokecherries in the box. We've found a grand patch of huckleberries. Let's go!"

She went back to the rig and then followed him up the hillside. Smitty was down on her knees, her pail beside her. "Practically got to go down under these bushes to pick," she said laughingly. Helen dropped down beside her and could smell a winey tang of crushed berries as she did so.

"Now look, you girls. I am going to do a bit of fishing," Bill said as he turned back toward the lakeshore.

Helen picked silently—thinking. The sun was warm on her shoulders, but without the burning quality it had held before the storm. She thought of bushfires again and remembered how Bill had gone to the lake for a pail of water to douse their picnic fire. She tasted the huckleberries and found them a sharp, keen flavour, but they set her teeth on edge just as the chokecherries had. She did not eat many. Smitty was humming a popular song. She leaned back on her heels and said, "Let's do this more often. I love the lake and the bush and the smell of berries."

Helen agreed, "Yes, it is fun." But she did not know then that never again would she smell the sharp tang of huckleberries without feeling faint and nauseated.

"And it pays dividends through the winter, when there is not fresh fruit around," Smitty continued to persuade her.

"How are we going to buy jars for all this jam?" Helen wondered.

"Mmm, I can just smell huckleberry pie right now," from Smitty.

They went on picking quietly for a long time, and Helen's fingers began to grow stiff. She was not at all sorry to hear Bill come thrashing though the bushes toward them. She jumped to her feet, ignoring the pair of silver trout he held up to their view, and shouted, "Johnny! Where is Johnny? Wasn't he with you?"

Bill stopped dead in his tracks. "Good Lord! I thought he was with you!"

"Oh Bill! Oh Bill! He has not been here since I started picking. I was sure he was with you."

Smitty put her hands to her mouth and called, "John-ee! John-ee!" Only the echo answered her.

They stood in silence—intent, listening. Then Bill cupped his hands and shouted, "John-ee! John-ee!" And again they listened to only the echo.

A broken sob escaped from Helen. "He has fallen into the lake!"

"I would have heard the splash," answered Bill. "It is so silent down there that every sound counts." He did not tell Helen what he knew to be true—there was less hope of finding the tiny tot in the underbrush than there was in the lake.

"Let's branch out," he commanded, his voice hoarse with anxiety. "Helen, you keep to the lakeshore so that you, too, don't get lost in the bush. Smitty, you skirt this hill. I will climb the ridge and listen. Both of you call, and I will listen up there for the answer if he should hear you."

The bush was now filled with sound, and it became a wail—"John-ee, John-ee!" But only echoes came back, again and again. Helen ran and stumbled all along the lakeshore, quickening her step every time a short log appeared on the beach or a rock rose in view, passing it with scarcely a glance when she came close enough to see what it was. She turned back again at a hail from Bill. Following his voice, she reached the clearing where he stood, Smitty beside him.

"We can't wait for darkness," he began without hesitation, "and we can't wait until he wanders too far away. I am going to take one of the sorrels and ride bareback to town to bring back a search party. You two girls hunt in a pair until I get back. Smitty, don't let Helen out of your sight." With that, he was gone.

"We'll start at the berry patch," Smitty spoke rapidly, her tone flecked with anxiety. "We'll work in a widening circle around it till we find him; a baby not yet three can't have wandered very far."

"They don't think I realize the danger," thought Helen, "but I do! Oh, I do!" Her feet were burning, her shins aching and full of thorns from the wild rose briars. She had misstepped on a rock and her ankle was swollen, but the weight of her heart outweighed all minor discomforts. "Johnny, Johnny, Johnny," her heart cried out. "All that was left to me of England, of home—my Johnny." Johnny, born amidst the crash of bombs falling on a large city, now lost in the solitude of the Canadian bush.

Smitty stumbled along by her side, praying inaudibly. Helen remembered gratefully the girl's genuine affection for the little boy and knew that Smitty would continue to search while there was the least vestige of hope.

Twilight descended with the suddenness it has in the North, but Helen saw nothing of the beauty of the sunset over the lake. Darkness gradually came down around them and Smitty ran back to the rig for Bill's long flashlight, and they continued their trek through the bush. Their circle had widened now to require climbing up the hillside, and walking became difficult. As darkness fell, the insects of the night came out more thickly, and mosquitoes swarmed up from the pools and eddies along the lakeshore to bedevil them, but Helen gave no thought to her own discomfort.

"My poor baby. My poor baby!" she panted aloud, and the incantation became a prayer. "My poor baby. My poor baby!" Her tone was beseeching.

Smitty slowed her pace because Helen found it increasingly hard to go on. At last—after a time that seemed endless—the bush was filled with sound around them. "Ahoy! Ahoy!" came from many voices.

"Smitty! Helen!" came from Bill and John Barnes. The girls stood still and answered, and soon the men climbed up to them. Mom Barnes and Mrs. Olson had come too. The rest were men from the seeding party—neighbours, all: Shaw, Jones, Olson, Barnes, and many others.

Smitty pointed out the area they had already searched. Lit lanterns were set swinging and long rays from torches stretched out, and the search began.

Helen was going to follow Bill, but Mom Barnes laid a restraining hand on her shoulder. "Just a minute, Honey! The men are going to need hot coffee; they have been in the fields all day. And we'll have to build a huge fire to guide them back. You stay with Mrs. Olson and me. Smitty, you had better rest too." But Smitty was already gone.

"Coffee!" Helen burst out, hysterically. "How could anybody think of coffee while he is out there, alone, in the dark?" Then she sank down on a crumbly log, exhausted, unable to go one step farther. She sat there as though in a trance, watching the long fingers of light reaching out, disappearing through the trees, and reaching out again. She sat listening with an intensity that almost drove her insane.

Mrs. Olson and Mom Barnes stood a little way off in the glare of the campfire they were making. Helen caught the sound of their voices. She heard the mention of Dr. Carney's name and the words, "as soon as he comes... best for her to be quiet." She blessed them for their understanding hearts. If they had forced her to speech, she would have screamed, so hard-pressed was she. Her eyes were wide open—unblinking, tense.

Toward dawn, the men began to drift back, one by one. Smitty came and sat on a log beside Helen, and Mom Barnes placed a cup of hot coffee in her hands. The fragrance reached Helen's nostrils, but her stomach tightened and nausea beset her; the women seemed to know this and they did not offer her any. Smitty rolled from the log and slept where she lay, mosquitoes humming about her. The legs of her slacks were torn to shreds and her shirt, also, was torn.

All the men had returned but three, she heard, and after each had eaten and had some coffee, they moved away again to commence the search once more. Hope was dead in Helen at last. Suddenly, Dr. Carney stood before her. "She is taking it bad, Doc," she heard Mom Barnes say quietly.

The doctor's face was deeply lined, and he leaned back on his heels. He had only then arrived, but Helen knew he had spent many sleepless hours. He squeezed her shoulder silently and then walked over toward the fire. He came back holding a steaming dipper in his hand, set it on the ground beside her, reached for her arm, and Helen felt the needle bite deeply. The physical pain was a relief.

She never knew how she came to be on a blanket, nor how many hours had passed, but the sun was well toward the hills in the west and there was bright daylight about her when she roused to the sound of shouts echoing and re-echoing against the hills and over the water. At first they meant nothing to her.

"All in! All in!"

"All in! All in!"

Then she saw the boy for the first time and a great light dawned on her. She had not even known he was in the search, for he was one of the three who had not come back for breakfast. He and Bill and John Barnes. Now he stood before the fire and his shoulder sloped down with the burden he held in his arms, and Johnny was wailing. It sounded to Helen very much like his first cry on the night of his birth. So far away, coming to her over the waves of anesthesia. She tried to get up but could not, and like that night, too, they came and laid him in the crook of her arm.

Helen closed her eyes and listened to Johnny's wail, hoping it would never stop. Then someone kneeled beside her and she opened her eyes to look into the tired face of Doc Carney. Yes, Doc was what they all called him. She heard him say to Mrs. Olson, "Warm milk, and feed him slowly." She turned to look at her baby and saw that his face was very swollen and inflamed, bleeding in places from the insect bites. It was hard to recognize him. "Ants are still crawling out of his clothes, I do declare!" Mom Barnes was saying as she bathed the poor little swollen face. "I wish I had a wee bit of baking soda to put in this water, but I never thought to bring any."

"Rod found him," Helen said to her. It was not a question. She was stating a fact, letting it sink into her own mind.

"Yes! God bless him! Down behind a log, with his foot twisted in a long vine, he had cried himself to sleep."

When they brought the warm milk, Helen sat up and cuddled her baby in her arms. Mrs. Olson held the cup and lifted a spoon to the bleeding lips. He drank greedily at first, eyes closed, but soon the head began to nod, sank back on Helen's shoulder, and he was asleep again—the deep sleep of contentment. They stood around her and watched him, this small object of their search.

Doc Carney and Bill were in a long, earnest conversation back of the crowd, and Smitty sat on the end of the blanket, chin in hand, relief from strain on every line of her face. Rod and John Barnes stood close to the fire drinking coffee, and there was a shrinking air about the boy, as though he wanted to escape attention.

"Mind that night?" he asked John Barnes. "The night the twins come? She sure was good to Ma. Ma sez she'll never forget it, but Ma can't do much. I guess God let me be the one to find that young 'un, eh?"

"You're right," John assured him. "I've heard tell there's a law of compensation."

Helen took in the scene as she sat with the baby on her knee. People grow close in times of stress and strain, and she suddenly felt very near to the people who stood around her. But as she glanced back over her shoulder toward the tall trees, whose tops reached up into the sunlight, and to the underbrush in the shadows, an involuntary shiver swept over her and she thought with longing of the neat fields, of the factory whistles blowing, and of crowds thronging the streets.

She knew that these twenty or so men standing about her were fairly representative of every family in the community, and she remembered Bill as he had stood on top of the ridge and said, "The last homestead between here and the North Pole." Her little son, her baby, had been lost—alone—in that vast expanse of uncharted countryside. She wondered if she was big enough to take it any longer.

Chapter Fifteen

*S*mitty preserved and made jam and jelly from the pails of berries that had been their day's picking, but Helen felt like throwing the lot away and left the smelly kitchen to Smitty for the whole day. She tenderly bundled Johnny into his coat and hat, and put him in his wagon alongside a box containing chicken, fresh butter, and homemade bread. She pulled the wagon along the old-wood road, crossed the little bridge, and climbed through the barbed wire fence at the corner by lifting Johnny through first and then the wagon. Following a trail through the bush, in a few minutes she came within sight of the log cabin and met the barking dogs with a word of rebuke, "Down pup, down! Behave yourself." She was too much the Englishwoman to be afraid of dogs.

As she pulled the wagon to stop in front of the door, an admiring voice greeted her.

"Gee, 'ou ain't scairt of them dogs? Most everybody is. You should've saw the Rawlin's man jump back in 'is car when they ran out at 'im!"

"Hello, Connie! No, I'm not afraid. How is Mother?"

"She's home," and the child took her thumb from her mouth and pointed inside. "I'm Ruthie."

"Oh, I'm sorry—Ruthie." As she knocked on the door, she called, "Hello!" She waited for the invitation and then walked in.

Mrs. Hughes sat in an old rocker in the middle of the room, her breast bared, nursing one of the twins. "Find a chair, Mrs. McElroy. I'll be through in a minute. The other one is asleep already."

"I wanted to see them. This one looks fine. He has gained weight, hasn't he?"

"Sure has, but Reggie is the biggest. Reggie and Roger, I called them. They go together, don't they?"

"Yes, they do. I like both of those names. How are you?"

"My back is bad. It's the washing as does it. You see, there are eight kids to wash for now, and the girls are not big enough to be much help yet. They do mind the babies for me, though."

"I don't see how you do it all."

"It's a case of have-to. It keeps Pa and Jimmy busy running the farm, it seems, and Rod goes to town for supplies for me. He was in the store the night Mr. McElroy went there to say the wee boy was lost. I was surely worried when he didn't come back, and Jimmy went to town to find him and the store was closed with a note on the door, so we knew where he was."

Helen paled even as she listened to the woman talk and she thought how very differently things might have ended. "That is one of the reasons I came over. Is Rod around?"

"No, Mrs. McElroy, he ain't; but just forget it anyhow. You know that out here we do things like that. Why, if that little lad had been one of our kids, your man would have been out there searching. We think nothing of such things. It can happen to anyone. That's one reason Westerners are like they are. We are all, more or less, dependent—one on another.

"This has been a bad year. The worst we've had round here; you will hear that on all sides. But in the good years, we all share and share alike. Come hunting season, the hunters split up the first deer or first moose they shoot. We are all mighty fond of wild meat, and we share until everybody has had some. Then and then only do we begin to freeze or can it."

Helen sat enthralled. She wanted to learn—to take it all in—and she had never felt so free to ask questions as she did with Mrs. Hughes.

She realized one strange thing: although it was recognized that the man of this family was a ne'er do well, everybody knew that his wife, labouring under great handicaps, was well-liked and welcomed everywhere. Their son, Rod, was also treated with respect and liking, almost affection, by the whole town's people. No class distinction here, Helen could see. A man was taken at his proven value.

She asked about the other children—their standing in the grade school, how they travelled to school, and so on.

"They walk. They have walked this many a year. Five miles is nothing to them kids, though I do wish we had a horse for them. But we haven't. Just an old work team."

"Bill is building a little two-wheeled cart for me so that I can drive old Bet to town. Something like that is what you want, isn't it?"

"Yes, it is. And Rod is a smart one with horses. He has a way with them, they say. Now, Jimmy is more of a mechanic, but it's horses for Rod. He says he will be a horse doctor when he grows up—thinks animals suffer just like people."

"I'm sure they do, too," agreed Helen.

Then they went on to talk about the babies. "We did not have a hospital in Cross Town till after my fourth was born. Doc Carney fought long and hard for that hospital, and at last he got it. All the rest were born at home, with only Pa to help me. I got along fine, though, till these twins. I'm sure I would have died but for you."

Just then, Johnny began to be restless in his wagon, and not wanting to bring him into the house, Helen prepared to leave. As she reached the screen door, the flies swarmed away from it. She stepped outside and came back with the box of food, and then she left hurriedly, before Mrs. Hughes could protest, calling back over her shoulder, "Send Rod over. Bill wants to see him."

When Bill took Rod out to the corral and asked him to pick out a horse for himself, the boy stood on one foot, then the other, and finally said, "It ain't no use, Mr. McElroy. Pa'd only sell it, like he did my turkeys I raised last summer and my five wee pigs I worked for and raised. He'll sell this horse, too, and that would kill me."

"Which one would it be, Rod?"

"That one—that young dapple there. She is not too long-legged and seems quiet. I think maybe she could be trained to haul the kids to school in a cart."

"Well, suppose I talked to your dad and told him I was going to let you break her for me, and then have you use her for a while for doing so? He would never dare sell my horse, would he?"

"No. He would never dare sell your horse—don't believe in hard feelings between neighbours."

"Well then, that's settled. But remember, when you get ready, come and get the bill of sale for her. What do you think you will call her?"

With shining eyes, Rod told him, "I've always thought I'd call a horse 'Bigenough,' and she's 'Bigenough' for me. Gosh, when I see Connie and Ruthie climbing into that cart.... I bet Jimmy'll be all heat up enough to help me make it, too!"

It was just about then that Lars Olson rode through the gate and, dismounting, led his horse over to the corral. "Fine bunch of young stuff you got here. What are you going to do with the stallion?"

"I'm going to have to sell him. I will only have about enough feed for four horses, and I'm short of cash."

"Well now, I might talk business with you on that point too, but I really came over to see if I could hire you and your combine to take the crop off my son's place, near my section. We thought he might be home when we seeded it, but the Air Force isn't releasing the boys very fast. I have all I can do to handle my own crop."

"I am mighty glad to be able to help you out, and it will help me too. Now, how do you want it worked—by the acre or on contract?"

"Now, look—that's up to you. I know I can trust you to give Sigvord a square deal. Ride over there tomorrow and look the place over, then come and let me know. Another thing— my outfit will be going at the same time on my place, so come over and eat with my crew. Tell the wife and her friend they are invited too. We would be very glad to have them."

With that, they walked toward the house and Helen invited Lars to stay for supper. She liked the tall, blond Scandinavian and was especially grateful to him because his coming had seemed to cheer Bill considerably. When he was gone, she asked Smitty, "Now what do we do? Do we take food along as they all did when they came here?"

"Oh no, Honey! They came to surprise you, and you were not expected to have the food on hand. Mrs. Olson will be glad just to have our help to feed the threshing crews."

Helen found that to be true. She had scarcely entered the kitchen and taken her coat off when Mrs. Olson dragged an old highchair from some remote corner for Johnny to sit in, gave him a cookie, and then stationed Helen over a long, hot griddle with an enamel pitcher of batter in her hand.

"Flapjacks," she explained. "I have fried so many now, I've lost count. But they are still going strong." Helen poured and turned them constantly until the batter was all gone, and her face was red and perspiring.

Then she graduated to a high stool beside the long oilcloth-covered kitchen table, and Mrs. Olson placed a wooden board before her, along with a huge bowl of crisp cabbage and a sharp knife. "Coleslaw," she was told and left to herself. She caught Smitty on the fly as the girl hastened between cellar and stove, and Helen received from her some detailed instructions on how to prepare cabbage for coleslaw. When the cabbage was shredded to her satisfaction, she set about rolling out pastry and lining pie-plates, then she sliced apples for the pies.

The long, cheery kitchen, with southern windows, was full of sunlight that streamed past the polka-dotted curtains. Mrs. Shaw was there, too. Mrs. Olson and Smitty bossed the job, while Grandpa Olson—very old and very deaf—sat in a corner churning the ice cream, saying nothing, apparently quite content to be an onlooker. When Helen caught his eye, she smiled, and he shouted at the top of his voice, "You have a fine young boy there!"

Thereafter, he was supreme favourite with Helen, and she let Johnny out of his highchair to sit beside the old man. The baby sat on the floor, and his eyes followed the gnarled, old hand as it turned the crank or lifted the lid to add more salt to the ice mixture.

"What's he do that for, Mummy? What's he?" Johnny demanded.

"To freeze ice cream, Lover."

"Can Johnny have some? Can he?"

"When it is frozen, you may."

"Is there a spoon in this house?"

"Yes, you can have some for dessert—not now."

"When's 'sert, Mummy? When's 'sert?"

"Oh... Darling...!"

"Mummy, this isn't my house, is it? Where did you leave my house, Mummy?"

"It will be there when we go home with Daddy tonight."

"Where's my daddy, Mummy?"

The men put an end to this endless interrogation as they came streaming through the back door, lined up at a long bench that held tin wash basins full of water, and washed the dust and grime of the fields from their faces before going through into the dining room.

"About one more gathering like this and I will begin to call all these people by their first names," Helen thought, for each man stopped to speak to the baby and his mother, or they nodded on their way through the kitchen. Bill was the last to arrive and as he walked through the door, Johnny stood back and eyed him uncertainly. Bill's face was so black that the eyeballs showed white in contrast, and his hair was thick with dust. He walked toward Helen and threatened to hug her, but she retreated in mock horror and pointed to the wash basins. He bent down and spoke to Johnny, but the boy held back from his open arms until he heard and recognized the voice. Then he ran to his father with a glad shriek.

Chapter Sixteen

If the summer was a dry one, September made up for it, for it ended with rainstorms that soaked and drenched the countryside. Fortunately, the crops were light and the fire and hail had left many hands for the work of harvest. But for a few of the crops left, all were safely in before the rains set in.

Rain swirled down from the mountains, blotting out the horizon, and presently it turned to sleet and then snow, blanketing the roads and fields and lending an air of lonely whiteness to the scene from Helen's window.

By the middle of October, winter had set in with an apparent determination to stay. It was with surprise, therefore, that Helen looked out on sunshine a few days later and listened to the steady drip, drip, of the snow as it thawed off the roof. Soon the roads were a soggy mess, good for neither wheels nor sleighs. Then they dried up again, and there were two weeks of lovely, clear weather that reminded her of the hot summer months again—warm summer days, cool night breezes.

The early frost had killed the flies and mosquitoes; walking or riding could be enjoyed in comfort. There was a sparkling clarity in the air that filled the lungs with goodness and gave a feeling of buoyancy of spirit—impossible in the hottest part of the year.

This, Helen was told, was Indian summer, and it was while she sat on the porch in a rocker, knitting woollen mitts for Bill, that a stranger entered the gate and walked up to the porch. Helen rose to greet the man, and he stretched out his hand, saying, "My name is Alexander Patrick, and when I met your friend Miss Smidt a few weeks ago, she suggested I call upon you. As you probably know, I am trying to rebuild the little church that was burnt down during the summer and to commence services again."

"Oh, yes," Helen replied. "Smitty has been telling me about you. She seems to be very interested in your endeavour to open the church for services hereabouts."

"I am making a tour of visitation to see how many would back the project, but of course, I had planned to call on you anyhow. You see, it was really because of Miss Smidt that I am here at all. Her brother and I were in college together, taking a refresher course after discharge from the services, and she wrote repeatedly, saying how desolate this district was of any kind of religious service, which made me determined to come here. The Mission Board was not at all enthusiastic, since the church had been burnt, so it is up to me to prove that I was not wrong in feeling that there was an opening here. Could you give me any idea of the response of your household?"

"Well, yes," Helen spoke slowly and thoughtfully. "I believe it would be favourable. I, myself, have felt a real need in my life since coming to this district and finding no organized service. Of course you know Smitty's opinion. I cannot, I'm afraid, speak for my husband, but I have heard him say that his mother was buried from that little church, and the funeral service for his dad was held there too. So I think old associations may draw him back there—more I cannot say. That leaves only my small son and he, of course, will go with me."

"You will be glad to hear, then, that I have made arrangements to use the schoolhouse in the meantime. Services will commence this coming Sunday at eleven o'clock. I will leave this announcement card with you."

"Thank you very much. Can you stay and have dinner with us?"

"I would be very glad to do so, though I must hurry away right afterward because I have other calls to make."

This meeting with the young preacher was the beginning of a long and pleasant friendship that ripened in the long winter months that followed. When Smitty came in, she stood, very quietly, looking at the young stranger, and before Helen could speak, Smitty recognized the visitor. Thereafter, he had a staunch and willing supporter to build again a church and a congregation.

Soon after this visit, the weather grew cold again; and soon, as Helen looked from the porch, she saw a whiteness, and the sun glinted and sparkled on the snow. The hills became silent—a great, austere backdrop. The sky grew gray and pregnant with snowy clouds.

"Will I ever get used to it?" she asked Smitty.

Smitty smiled her wise smile and said, "Before spring thaws, it will be a part of you."

Disbelief filled Helen's heart. If truth were told, a fear hung over her—a terror of the unknown vastness that seemed more formidable than ever in its snowbound immensity. A foreboding, perhaps, that was only a throwback to the night of suspense she had endured when her baby was lost in the bush by the lakeshore.

Helen no longer remembered the primitive beauty that surrounded the crystal-clear lake. No longer did she remember the enchanted whispering of the pines along the lakeshore; rather, she thought of the myriad insects that buzzed by night and remembered the distance, the hopelessness, of the place, and she felt hemmed in by it—by the blanket of snow.

Bill was planning a trip back into the bush at the far end of the lake, waiting only until the ice should be firm and solid enough for man and team. As yet, though, the snow fell soft and thick, lying in drifts and mounds by fences and ditches. The temperature was above zero, with water still running in rivers and creeks, and only slush edging the lakeshore. He planned to build a caboose on his sleigh and to make an extended stay in the bush, selecting timber to replace the buildings that had been lost in the fire. He wanted to get out some saw logs too, so that he would have some lumber on hand for flooring and roofing.

Well aware that he had a heavy winter's work ahead of him, he set about gathering materials to build his caboose in the interval before freeze-up. He had obtained a sturdy set of sleighs in a horse trade with Lars Olson, and some lumber from Pop Barnes on a promise to pay when his own logs were sawed up. He sent to the city for heavy canvas and several pieces of

Plexiglas from the War Assets Corporation, and when these arrived, he started work on the caboose.

When he had it finished, it looked like an elaborate covered wagon on sleighs with a stout canvas roof and walls. Small windows were in the front and sides, and a narrow slit was cut below the front window, through which the lines were inserted. A narrow stovepipe rose up through the roof, proclaiming a stove within, and a door was fitted tightly at the back. Inside, there were benches along one side, and in front, a small table—on hinges, so it could be dropped flat against the wall—before a tiny, airtight heater.

Bill knew from experience that such equipment, while very simple, was indispensable on a stay in the bush in below-zero weather. To say that Helen regarded his preparations with lack of enthusiasm was to put it mildly. Yet Bill could not be prevailed upon to abandon his plans.

"Why, Honey!" He looked at Helen with blank amazement in his eyes when she protested. "I must make this logging trip. You know we need the logs for building, and there is no other way to get them in this country. Besides, I am looking forward to it. I will take my .30-30 rifle and perhaps bring you back some venison. There is good hunting up there at the end of the lake. I must get my licence before I go."

"Bill! Bill!" Helen argued. "Suppose you have an accident—shoot yourself or some such thing. You will be so far away from help, and we would never know what happened to you for... a month, maybe." She stopped with a catch in her voice.

Bill laughed, and then he pulled her close to him, realizing for a moment how serious she was. "Know something, Honey? I believe you love your old man," he teased her.

But Helen's fears were very real, and anything she could do to delay Bill's departure was a welcome relief to her. It was with this in mind that she started coaxing one morning to be taken over to visit Mrs. Shaw.

"You know, Bill, I promised—when she came here to visit me and then again at Mrs. Olson's. I would like to meet Nelly Shaw. She has never been to any of the gatherings or even to church services. I feel rather sorry for her because of some remarks I have heard. How about it?"

Bill was just a little surprised, for Smitty had told him of Mrs. Shaw's outburst, and he thought that Mrs. Shaw's sour disposition would have repelled rather than attracted his sensitive, young wife.

"How about going to Olson's?" he inquired.

"No. I see Olsons often—at church and almost every other place I go. Mrs. Barnes, too. And I can walk to see Mrs. Hughes. No, I want to visit the Shaws. I have a guilty conscience about not doing it sooner."

"Well..." he said, somewhat doubtfully. "You are the boss."

Smitty decided to ride into town with some letters she had written, so they took the small cart, now mounted on sleighs and painted a bright red, which looked exciting against the white snow. Bundled up in a coat, leggings, and a cap with warm earflaps that Smitty had made for him, Johnny looked like a little red elf with rosy cheeks and shining, brown eyes.

"Where did you get those brown eyes?" Bill teased him, pinching the dimpled chin.

"From Mummy. She gave 'em to me." Johnny had the answer down pat; he had heard so many people say, "He has his mother's eyes."

"No, she did not. I have brown eyes too, you know." Bill pretended to pout, and the baby was delighted.

"Johnny—Smitty's boy," he asserted.

They climbed into the cart with blankets around the heated rocks at their feet, though that almost seemed unnecessary as the sunshine was so bright.

"You are going to drive, Madam, because Smitty and yourself will have to go for supplies when I am in the bush. Old Bet is fool-proof, but I want to see if you know 'Gee' and 'Haw' well enough to suit me."

They had four miles to drive and old Bet travelled slowly, jogging contentedly along. She needed very little guidance and could have been led by a child. She stood perfectly still when her lines were dropped, and turned right or left at the words "Gee" or "Haw" without any pull on the lines at all. Bill was satisfied that Helen had a safe means of conveyance and hoped old Bet's days would be long and many—at least until he was able to afford an old car or light truck. He knew Helen could drive.

The Shaw house was a square, unpainted frame building with a long porch running the length of the house. It stood in a wide, cleared field, and the barns were comfortably close to the back door. Not a tree or shrub had been left standing in the clearing close to the buildings, giving the place a bleak, unfriendly appearance.

"Prairie people," Bill explained, "nearly always root out the bush like that. Not used to trees, I guess. I don't like the idea myself, but I have to agree that it pays in a fire year, like this has been."

Two large dogs ran out barking and snapping at old Bet's heels, but she plodded nonchalantly along and drew to a standstill in front of the door. The door swung open, and Mrs. Shaw came out on the porch. "Down, Bud. Down, Tex," she called crossly to the dogs, and they slunk away and out of sight at the back of the house.

"Miserable things," she grumbled. "Come in, won't ye?" This she said to Helen, and it was more in the nature of a querulous command than an invitation. To Bill she said, "Dad's over at the barn. Take your horses over there if you're staying."

Bill carried Johnny up the front steps and into the front room of the big farmhouse, then he went out and led old Bet off to the barn.

"Take your things off and make yourself comfortable," Mrs. Shaw said as she went around the room picking up newspapers and straightening cushions. "We wasn't expecting visitors, so you must take us as you find us."

"Why, your place is fine. Mine is always mussed up with Johnny's playthings."

"Oh, I know what that is like too. Raised a family myself, though I can't say as they ever had many toys. Don't hold with throwing money away on useless stuff. Three boys and one girl, I had."

"Yes, you mentioned Nelly once. I would like to meet her. Is she home?"

Mrs. Shaw looked suspiciously into Helen's face, but apparently satisfied with what she saw there, she nodded her head toward the kitchen. "She's back there," she said, "making pies for supper. Good worker, Nelly is, but headstrong—powerful headstrong. Like her father that way. Little children is little trouble, I say; big children, big trouble. When they are small, they step on your toes. When they are big, they step on your heart." She sighed deeply, and Helen felt a depressing atmosphere about the house.

"Have you lived here long?" Helen asked.

"A good many years," was the reply. "We came from the dustbowl in Saskatchewan in the early thirties, homesteaded this land, cleared it, made a fine farm of it. Years of hard work." And she sighed again.

Just then, a girl came from the kitchen on her way to the bedroom that opened off the living room. Her mother stopped her with the wave of a hand and a nod toward Helen. "Meet my daughter, Nelly, Mrs. McElroy," she said. Nelly nodded and Helen rose from her chair and held out her hand.

"I'm very glad to meet you, Nelly," she said.

There was just the slightest hesitation before Nelly moved toward her, hand outstretched. "I've heard of you, Mrs. McElroy, from Mother," Nelly said, her soft voice a sharp contrast to the grumbling, querulous tone of her mother's. She had fine blue eyes—wide—beneath dark, sharply outlined eyebrows, but her face was unusually plain, and her skin brown and coarsened, as though she had lived the outdoor life of a man. Her hair was pulled straight back with no pretense at care or styling. She was short and stout, almost square in outline, and Helen was startled to see that she was in a well-advanced stage of pregnancy.

The most charitable observer could not have truthfully said her appearance was attractive, but there was something about Nelly that held Helen's attention. There was a self-confidence, a clarity of thought in the girl's face and speech that won her admiration. When Nelly turned, after a few remarks, and went into the bedroom, Helen wished she had stayed to better their acquaintance. Mrs. Shaw was rambling on, and Helen gave her attention because she was speaking of her daughter.

"She's not married, you know. Nearly broke her father's heart; though, as I say, it was his fault from the start. I never wanted him to hire that Pole with the dark, handsome looks. Never trusted him from the first. Had his finger off at the knuckle—trigger finger, too—and that looked suspicious to me, because he was call-up age. Just like our two eldest. Nelly never 'peared to pay no attention to him, but I did not like him on the place even. 'You're plain,' I told her over and over, 'but Pa'll fix it up somehow that you get a man when this war is over and the men come back.'

"She never said a word. Didn't seem to care, either, and then this happened. No, she won't marry him. Her father said he would fix them up on a quarter-section, start them with some young stock and some money in the bank, but Nelly would have none of him. Doesn't want a husband, she says—just a child. Did you ever hear the like? Wants Dad to keep all his promises and let her live on the place alone, farm it herself. Well, we don't know what to do. I'm near crazed. The Shaws have always had a good, honest name."

"Mother is behind the times!" They had not heard Nelly approach, but she stood quietly beside the round table and looked directly at Helen. "She thinks a woman must have a man to run the place. Now, I have helped Dad since I could walk. There is nothing on a farm I cannot do, and if he is going to give me a farm, why should I have to share it with someone else?

"I have earned the money he promises me, for I have worked hard for Mother and Dad and received only my room and board and the most inexpensive clothing in return. They can well afford to help me get a comfortable start now, and I can be a great help to them, living so close, in their old age. But Mother does not see that. She thinks I must have a man—even someone she distrusts and dislikes—to make me respectable. Well," turning to her mother, "it is my life and I am going to live it my way. If you and Dad cannot see your way to keep the promises you made to me years ago, I have other plans."

Helen saw stark fear in the eyes of the mother as she watched the girl make her way to the kitchen.

"Nelly is right, Mrs. Shaw. This is a modern world, and why should she marry a man she does not love? Why, Nelly has courage of a most unusual sort. Are you not proud of her?"

Mrs. Shaw looked up in surprise. "You think people won't talk?" she asked tearfully.

"Of course they will," Helen warned her, "but it is too late to prevent that now, even if Nelly did get married right away. And if Nelly does not mind, why should you? You are her mother. Can you not trust her to make a wise decision?"

Mrs. Shaw sat—silent, thinking deeply—and Helen went to the kitchen in search of Johnny. Nelly was sitting in a rocker beside the stove, the little boy on her knee, a faraway expression in her eyes. Johnny was contentedly munching a cookie. Helen pulled up a chair and sat down beside them, and Nelly smiled a welcome. The spicy smell of apple pie came from the oven.

Helen looked around the kitchen. It was evidently Nelly's domain, and the gloominess that pervaded the rest of the house refused to penetrate here. The cheerful gingham curtains were pulled well back, tied with bright bows, and the sunlight shone through clean panes, unhindered. Little pots of cheeky red geraniums perched on the windowsill, and in front of the window stood a square wooden table. The table-top was scrubbed clean and white. No cover graced it, but a tiny pot of green creeper stood in the centre. Long wooden benches stood on either side of the table, completing the dining arrangements. The tall black stove was polished until it gleamed, reflecting sunlight from the windows. Along the wall, near the white sink, hung neat rows of pots and pans. The pump at the sink was painted a cheerful red. The bare wooden floor was scrubbed as clean as the table top.

Helen decided the room was very like the girl—plain, clean, but above all, warm and welcoming. They sat side by side listening to Johnny's chatter, and words seemed unnecessary to cement their friendship.

Yet suddenly, Helen found herself talking volubly, unloading her heart. For the first time, she went over the details of the night Johnny was lost in the bush. She expressed aloud her horror of the unknown distances, and then she began to talk of home—Dad, Sue, Aunt Min. Helen scarcely realized that Nelly seldom spoke a word; she listened—genuinely, deeply, sincerely—not offering advice.

They both started to their feet in surprise when the back door opened and the men stomped into the kitchen, bringing a draught of cold air with them.

Mr. Shaw's mouth dropped and his eyes opened wide. Never, in all the years since Nelly had grown up, had he come into his kitchen at mealtime to find the table unset—no food around. And never had he heard Nelly laugh as she did at the surprise on his face and at her own forgetfulness. Come to think of it, he had never heard Nelly laugh at all. He looked at Helen, expecting to see someone very different, but he saw only a slender, brown-eyed girl with a flushed, guilty look on her face.

Chapter Seventeen

When old Bet turned in at the gate, Helen breathed the fragrant pine smoke as it blew down from the chimney. Smitty had lit the tall Aladdin lamp, and she put it on a table near the window and ran out to meet them. The light streamed through the doorway, across the porch, and out onto the snow.

Home looked good—warm and cozy—after only a day away from it. Helen drank in its comfort and security. She still carried with her the glow of a new friendship well begun.

Smitty clutched Johnny to her with a hunger that bespoke her fondness of him, having been parted for only the day. "The milking is done, and all the chores finished," she called to Bill as he made his way to the barn.

"What would we do without Smitty?" Helen asked as she stretched her legs and climbed the steps to the porch. Yet even as she spoke, she knew there was a difference in their relationship, a difference she did not care to analyze. "My toes are freezing in spite of the hot rocks; but I get my diploma, I guess. Bill admits I can drive a horse—even grants me permission to drive to town alone now. But oh, there is no place like home! I am so glad to be back."

She followed Smitty, who was carrying the sleepy little boy, through the door and into the warm living room, where a roaring fire burned in the big heater. Bill came in from the barn, stamping his feet and clapping his hands together.

"Well, the thermometer is going down," he enthused, "below zero by morning and freeze-up in the next few days. Then, away to the lake for me. Now, Helen, don't pout. You can't grumble after I have spent a whole day pink tea-ing with you."

But Helen dropped her eyes to the floor thoughtfully. She had, somehow, discovered a new abundance of courage within herself in the last few hours. This was the West, where men were men and women were their kind.

Next day, she set to work to bake bread and beans and to pack a grub box for the caboose. Rising one morning, she saw Bill start up the trail by the old-wood road. The temperature was so low that the sleighs screeched in protest as they passed over the frozen snow.

Breathing was made difficult by the intense cold, though Bill rode in the heated caboose where a fire burned in the little heater, leaving a wisp of smoke along the trail behind him. He headed for a stand of timber on the farthest shore of the lake. He had many miles to travel before reaching the break in the shoreline, where he then dropped onto the ice. While going up the centre of the lake, he was at the mercy of the icy north wind as it whistled down over the pine trees that fringed the shore.

He was dressed in a wind-proof parka with wolverine fur close to his face, duffel mitts inside the leather ones on his hands, and mackinaw trousers. He had still more care for his horses, for under their harness they wore heavy burlap blankets, pinned with huge frost-covered pins. Their chests and shoulders were protected with a canvas shield—up under their martingales and snapped to the hames. Bridles, blankets, harness, and horses' flanks bore a coat of feathery hoar frost before they had travelled too many miles.

On he went—now riding in the caboose, now trotting alongside—lines held tightly in hand, stamping his feet to keep them warm inside the moccasin rubbers. It was while he was in the caboose, letting the horses jog along at their own rate of speed, that he saw a black streak dart across the trail ahead of the team. A wolf.

Instantly, the horses were like wild things; Bill rose to his feet, pulling the lines till the muscles strained in his arms in an attempt to hold them, his feet spread apart, head pressing against the canvas roof. On they went, running and stumbling into the snow drifts, breaking trail as they went. Suddenly the right-hand line snapped against the pressure, but the left still held, and to this Bill hung on with all his might.

The team now ran in a circle, always veering to the left, and when Bill saw this, he acted quickly. Completing the circle once more, he dropped the line and jumped from the caboose, the door swinging open behind him. Halfway around the circle—for the horses continued to follow the trail they had broken in the deep snow—he saw the stove come flying through the door, burning wood hissed down into the snow.

When the sorrels reached him, he sprang to the nearest horse and, hanging onto it, closed his hand tight across the nostrils, shutting off the frenzied animal's breath. A few steps further and the smothered horse stumbled and fell in the trail, bringing his teammate down with him.

Bill clung tight until their terror had subsided, hoping against hope that the flailing hoofs would not reach him. When they had quietened down and he could lead them behind him along the trail, he picked up the little heater and reinstalled it in the caboose. He inspected the grub box to see what had spilled, and then he fixed the broken line—with great difficulty, because his hands were almost frozen as he bared them to the frosty air.

Once more the trek began, down the wind-swept lake in the direction of the setting sun. The heavy caboose dragged, and the horses breathed audibly in the stillness of the frozen twilight. There was only the yapping of a coyote in the distance. Darkness fell and then the northern lights flashed out, lightening the sky with glory and splendour, with their myriad colour and fluid movement.

Bill was cold and hungry when he reached the shoreline and made the steep ascent into the tall timber, where he unharnessed his horses and fed them in the shelter of the big trees. Then he lit a fire in the caboose stove and toasted the frost out of his sandwiches. Soon he had a pot of coffee boiling and bacon frying, and he ate hungrily before he unrolled his bedroll and settled down for the night.

The frost came through the floorboards and through the canvas of his eiderdown. The wind howled, and the trees moaned and bent before it. A long, lonely howl reached him from the far end of the lake and he thought of the horses, securely tied and blanketed for the night. He turned over on his side and slept.

Back at the homestead, Helen stood at her bedroom window and listened to the wind scream around the house and howl down the chimney. She heard the sounds in the night— listened to the horses moving in the makeshift barn near the new corral, listened to a kitten mewing on the porch—and felt depressed and frightened in spite of all her brave resolutions to do better.

Sleep was impossible. She poked around the room and covered Johnny with an extra blanket. Then she went to the back door, to let the kitten in off the porch, and went through the living room, adding a long piece of cordwood to the heater. It roared and crackled and sent out a grateful heat so that Helen moved back and sat down in a big chair, at a short distance from it. There, she sat in the darkness and listened to the wind and the roar of the fire, to Smitty's steady breathing in her bedroom, and to the occasional sharp crack of the big logs in the walls as they expanded with frost. Helen knew the thermometer was dropping, knew the snow would be flying again before morning, and knew Bill would be gone for days that could lengthen into weeks.

"If I am not back in three weeks, begin to worry—not before," had been his parting words.

She could not expect a letter or word of any kind from him, as he was well off the beaten trails. If he met with accident—was injured in any way—he had no means of sending word to her. Even if he could reach his horses and turn them loose, they would head for the range in the foothills, not for the homestead.

Helen sat, brooding, and forgot to appreciate the warmth she basked in. She forgot to think of a pantry and cellar well-stocked with foods too bountiful to be wished for in other parts of the world. She disregarded the comfort and good taste that surrounded her in the very room where she sat. Was this the kind of life she had wanted? Long, lonely evenings on an isolated farm with the nearest neighbours one mile one way, three the other—no telephone, no friendly lights outside, very little choice of companionship.

Then she thought of Smitty. Smitty, who had changed, strangely, inexplicably—a quiet, exciting, secret kind of change. Smitty, who attended church services regularly and cheerfully every Sunday, asked very little from life, loved the farm, and rarely confided in anyone.

Helen thought of John Barnes; his cheerful, confident attempt to win Smitty's interest, and his air of discouragement when she failed to respond. Then Helen remembered Smitty's concern for Bill's every comfort, her defence of his every wish. She remembered the secret looks of understanding between them. Remembrance came of Bill's tender attitude toward the girl who had been a real friend to his wife in those trying early days. She thought of the long times they spent together in the fields and about the buildings, the fencing, and making barns winter-proof.

Jealously, she asked herself, "What did they talk about through the long hours? Did they work separately?" She wondered. Why did Bill discuss every move he made toward the improvement of the place with Smitty instead of her? Could it be that she had not proved a very interested listener? Did Bill really prefer a Canadian farm girl, and did he regret having married an Old Country one from the city?

Thus Helen tortured herself through that stormy night with questions she could not answer, and when Smitty arose in the morning to milk and care for the animals, she found Helen haggard and distraught, in no mood to talk or be comforted.

Smitty knew, in some vague way, that Helen no longer loved or trusted her, and she felt an uneasiness in the atmosphere that boded no good. Yet, she knew that to leave was impossible. She felt herself held there by secret ties and hope; too, she knew Bill had a hard winter of work scheduled ahead of him if the logs were to be hauled and the new barns set up before spring breakup and seeding began.

Smitty persuaded herself that Helen was suffering homesickness, and she endured the long silences and embarrassments patiently. She contrived to spend long hours with the animals and chickens, and she made frequent trips to town on the saddle horse, sometimes only being on-hand to do the morning and evening chores.

The girls grew further and further apart, and Helen was left lonely and discouraged. The pangs of homesickness became so acute as to be an actual illness with her. The longing for her own folk and her overseas friends became a voiceless ache that lived with her by day and by night. She spent many hours in writing long, emotional letters to them, and it was well that she had this outlet. Mrs. Kennedy and Ma Kelly received mail from her frequently. Ma Kelly, sensing the extreme unhappiness of her friend, tried to persuade her to "pack and come home for a holiday."

Bill came and went with loads of logs throughout the long winter, working his team to the utmost of their endurance. He felt deep frustration at his failure to make Helen happy and content, and he was thrown more and more on Smitty to seek encouragement for the enormous tasks on hand.

One evening, a near climax was reached when he had arrived home, sleighs piled high with a load of huge pine logs. Man and horses were covered with frost, sending smoky wreaths into the air. When Smitty heard the sleigh grinding down the hill behind the house, she looked toward Helen, who sat rapt in thought and made no motion toward the door or window. Hesitating momentarily, Smitty jumped up and reached for the gas lantern, and pumping and lighting it, she ran with it to the door and on out to the gate.

Bill leaned down to Smitty from the logs and took the lantern from her hands, thanked her cheerfully, and then went on to the barn to feed the team before he would enter the house to eat and warm himself.

Helen still sat, ignoring his arrival, so Smitty set about getting a hot meal on the table, well-knowing the hungry appetite of a man returning from the bush. Bill came in, puffing and blowing as the warm air struck his lungs, and made his way to the warm stove.

"Perfect set of logs," he announced enthusiastically. "That's the last of the set for the big barn. The rest will be much easier to haul—smaller."

Still, Helen seemed sunk in her own thoughts—unapproachable. Smitty stood silently, and Bill looked toward her. Their glances met and locked above Helen's head. It was then that Helen looked up for the first time, only to hastily lower her eyes again, as though to give them more privacy.

Supper was finished in a tense silence. Bill dressed to go out again, then, bending over Helen's chair, he said, "Like to come out and look over my perfect set of logs, Helen? The moon is coming up, so you will see how big they are. Why, I'm so proud of them."

Helen shook her head and, picking Johnny up from his highchair, walked with him into the bedroom. Smitty washed the dishes, put the food away, and then she, too, dressed for the out-of-doors and made her way to the barn.

Bill was standing between the sorrel team currying the mottled sweat from their flanks when she entered. He laid down his curry comb and walked toward her, put his hands on her shoulders, and turned her face to the lantern light. Her face looked so fresh, so fair. There was an air of wholesomeness, of good sense, about Smitty that won a man's approval. His frustration over Helen almost swamped him as he stood there in the moist heat of the barn, the smell of horseflesh strong in his nostrils, the dry dust of grain in his throat.

He looked at the blue-eyed, fair-haired girl he had learnt to lean on so heavily. He would have pulled her toward him, but she resisted and opened her mouth to speak. Gently, he put his fingers beneath her chin and closed her mouth, leaving the unspoken words hanging in the air between them.

"Smitty," he said, standing there in the lantern light, "I've licked 'em all. I've hunted 'em down. Out there in the clean, cold air—in the bush—alone night and day, using my own strength to saw and chop and fell those giants of the woods. Alone with my own horses in my own country, I've hunted them all down and licked 'em. You know what I mean, don't you, Smitty?"

His glance probed deep, pleading for understanding, and she returned his gaze with an honesty that matched his own. This man who stood before her had come to mean so much to her. For him and his, she had left her work, had neglected her family, had worked for little or nothing as his fortunes fluctuated. Now he stood before her and searched her soul. How far would she go for him? Would she tear her heart out and lay it at his feet—sacrifice her own ambitions? Would she fight his battles further with him? For him? Where did their future lie?

She listened as he went on. "Those blank spaces—those stretches of darkness I could not explain—they were always there. I could not talk about them. I could not turn and face them. And they would creep up, reach out for me. I would wake from my sleep drenched in horror, and I could not look back at them, Smitty!

"I went right up to where Joe Sabrinski was lying on the beach with a hole in his side and his leg lying further up the beach. That leg looked funny, with the pant leg rolled down like a cuff just below the knee, and the ragged, bleeding end sticking out. I got down on my knees and stuffed my shirt into the hole in his side, and when he asked me, I handed him his rifle—loaded—and I turned my head while he pulled the trigger. Then I turned back and covered him.

"Yes, Smitty, I went back through the darkness and I lived it over again, and now I will never be afraid of Joe Sabrinski again. I know I did right when I gave him his rifle.

"I went back and I jumped over the dyke again, when the shell was screaming close, and I fell on top of them again, sticky with their own blood—warm, but dead. I stayed with them down there till the shelling stopped, and then I climbed out and I rolled and rolled. I could not walk, for there was a fire burning in my leg and a screaming in my ears. I don't know where my feet were; I never felt them at all. I put my hand up and blood had dried on my face—my own, or theirs? It was caked and it pulled my skin, and I could still hear the screaming. Was I screaming? Or was it only them?

"Then I remembered the boats, only three of them and one was sunk before our eyes. Men kept coming, crowding the beaches, ever leading on, to get across before dawn broke.

"After the one boat was sunk, the second began to fill with water, but the men kept trying to climb in, so the officer stood at the end with his gun. They swam after it, halfway across.

"I saw them come over the sides, those same fellows who had fought to get on. We were left behind, and we were the luckiest after all.

"I hunted them out—those shadows that I had refused to face—and I looked at them, and they aren't there any more, Smitty! I've faced them and in doing that, I've beaten them down. And I can face this too! I'll battle it, and it will work out alright. My luck won't change now. But don't leave, Smitty. Don't leave yet, for that is what you were going to say, wasn't it?"

That was the way Helen found them when she opened the barn door, and he was saying, "Don't leave, Smitty. Don't leave yet," and they were looking into each other's eyes, deeply.

Helen closed the barn door softly, and she went back toward the house. The night was colder—bitter. Her heart was empty—cold too. Why had she not gone with Bill to see to the logs? What contrariness made her act the way she did? Now she did not even have hope left. She was more alone than when she had first reached Canada.

Late that night, or early in the morning, she slipped from his side in their bed and, walking noiselessly through the kitchen into the living room, she stopped before the front door. Reaching high to the pair of antlers above the door, she took down a .22 rifle and, opening the door, she went out into the night.

She pulled her kimono tight around her but shivered in the biting cold as she made her way in the moonlight along the trail, up the old-wood road to the top of the ridge, stumbling in her high-heeled slippers as she went. She found an old tree stump and sat down, looking over the wide expanse of country and down the darkened trail to the lakeshore. The trail that Bill had travelled almost every week. She sat on the tree stump, shivering. She let the gun slip to the ground unnoticed. When the moon slipped behind a cloud, she rose and turned back down the trail toward the house. She didn't see the figure who stepped back into the bush by the trail side, picked up the gun, and then followed her down the trail and into the house.

In the morning, Bill saw the gun on the living room table. "Who was fooling with my rifle?" he demanded and snapped it open. "Why, the shells are gone. I'm sure I left it loaded and hung it up."

"You must have emptied it the day you went after the prairie chicken on the hillside," said Smitty in a soothing voice. "I might have left it down when I dusted it."

That day, a storm blew down from the hills and roared over the old house in a frenzy that threatened to tear it apart. The logs cracked and groaned and gathered themselves a coating of hoar frost. It was well that Bill was home, for Helen would have been crazed had he been away in the bush. As it was, she paced the length and breadth of the house, measured the peeled log wall with her eyes, and looked through the window in terror.

Bill kept the big heater loaded with cordwood. Smitty minded the baby in the kitchen, leaving the house only to milk and collect the eggs before they froze in the nests. The day wore on, and night descended with a blackness that could be felt, filled with a swirling, roaring of wind.

Smitty put the baby to bed, and the rest of the household was about to retire after a long dull evening, strained conversation, and an atmosphere almost as thick and angry as the storm without.

Helen was still pacing the floor when, suddenly, she stopped dead in the middle of the room. Something seemed to drag across the porch and then thump against the door. The sounds were muffled by the roar of the storm and she stood, listening, trying to pick up the sound again. Bill noticed her gaze fixed in horror on the door, and in one stride he was at it, pulling it open to swing it wide.

It was a heavy, double-plank door, but in spite of its weight and strength, the wind, stronger still, nearly tore it from his grasp. Papers and books rustled in the room, some photographs came tumbling down from a shelf. The curtains blew wildly.

As Bill opened the door, the figure of a boy stumbled in, half leaning against the door, then slipping to the ground in utter weariness. There he sat, his back against the open door, his head bent down by weakness. The boy's face was so cut and bruised that Helen didn't recognize him at once, but she well-knew the torn plaid shirt, the patches on the denim overalls, and the worn windbreaker that had once been Bill's.

"Rod!" she almost screamed, and she ran to his side and, with Bill's help, got him into the room and shut the door. As Helen knelt beside Rod—who leaned against her, his head lolled onto her shoulder—she looked up, and for the first time in days, her eyes met Smitty's. "Warm water," she said.

Soon Helen was bathing the bruised and bleeding face, while Bill pulled off the frozen moccasins the boy was wearing and began to massage his half-frozen feet. While they worked on him, Rod lost all consciousness, and it was not until he lay on a couch by the heater, warm again and wrapped in blankets, that he recovered enough to know where he was. Then he grew excited and tried to talk, but they gently pushed him back and fed him hot soup that Smitty brought.

When at last he was allowed to talk, the boy told his story. Bill listened in growing fury. Hughes had taken the horse, just as Rod had predicted he would.

"I don't believe no fool yarn about him not being yours," he had said to Rod.

The horse had been sold and, after a week in Cross Town, Hughes had returned loaded down with several crocks of moonshine. As had happened so often before, once in a drunken rage, he had picked on the boy whom he had wronged. The children would be facing bitter weather in their five-mile walk to school, for the little caboose that Bill had built for them to ride in had been sold, too.

Goaded beyond endurance, Rod had turned on his father, only to be beaten unmercifully by the tall, lean man.

"He took a martingale to me, and when that broke, he reached for a crosstree," Rod told them between gasps that were almost sobs. "Then Ma opened the door for me, and I ran out and he could not follow because of the storm."

"Is your mother safe?" asked Bill in alarm.

"He has never hit Mother yet. He knows what side his bread is buttered on, I guess. And anyhow, he was all wore out licking me."

Chapter Eighteen

The Christmas season crept up on them with the speed it usually does, and Helen knew near contentment again as she found herself busily engaged in caring for Rod, for it was many weeks ere he was up and around again. A respiratory infection set in, and the boy had suffered shock from the beating he had received and his super-human struggle through the storm.

Only Doc Carney's skill and the miracles of modern medicine had saved him. Helen refused to allow him to be taken to hospital and she'd nursed him tenderly herself. His mother came and spent part of a day with him, and reassurance about her well-being was as good as a tonic to the boy.

"I was sure I was sending him to his death when I opened the door and pushed him out into the storm," she told Helen, "but at least he had a chance out there, and I knew he would crawl here if he could. He thinks so much of you."

Indeed, it was almost adoration that Helen saw in the young boy's eyes as she bent over his bed from day to day. This helped to restore her self-confidence, and gave her a new hope of finding a useful place in the community. It helped her, too, to find a new level on which she and Bill could work together, for they both felt the urge to help Rod in his misfortune; they had in common a sense of gratitude to the boy who had saved their baby's life.

One day, Bill made a trip to a ranch halfway between Moosewell and Cross Town, and when he came back, he carried in his saddlebag a gunnysack of fine quality lamb's wool. This set Smitty to reminiscing about the season of wool spinning that was an annual event in the German-settled district where she had been born. Bill asked for details, and she drew a clear picture of an old German spinning wheel. He took the picture and disappeared into the workshop he had built for himself and, several days later, walked through the back door carrying a perfect working model.

For the first time in their acquaintanceship, Helen saw Smitty give full reign to her emotions and watched her as she went into ecstasies of joy over the instrument. The thought struck Helen that perhaps Smitty had spells of homesickness too, but she was much more preoccupied in thinking how anxious Bill had been to give Smitty pleasure.

Immediately, Smitty took up a position in the corner of the kitchen between the stove and the window. Yard after yard of beautiful, fine wool flowed from her fingers at an almost impossible rate. Her face was flushed with pleasure, and it was hard to tell whether her satisfaction sprang from the joy of creative ability or from thankfulness for the quality and quantity of the wool. Probably a mixture of both, Helen decided, and she had to admit that Smitty had reason to be proud of her handiwork. Helen wound the spun wool into skeins and washed it in soft, soapy water until it reached a fluffy whiteness. Then, together, they chose some cheerful dyes—red, green, soft baby blue and the palest pastel pink, and some quiet gray for socks. But most of it they left the snowy white that was its natural shade. Some was wound in two-ply, some three and four.

Then they began to knit. They solicited the aid of Mom Barnes and Mrs. Olson, for their program of gift-making was ambitious, to say the least. They worked at knitting and knitting, day-in and day-out, for weeks on end. They taught Rod to knit and kept him busy until he complained that it was the "knittingest" place he had ever seen.

The first presents to be finished were parcelled and sent off to England: a gay scarf and gloves for Sue, a pair of socks for Dad, mittens and a shopping bag for Aunt Min. These had first place because of the distance they had to travel.

Then came mittens, scarves, and socks for all the members of Smitty's family, and Helen went to extra trouble to see these were neat and well done, because Smitty had been so kind about the gifts to England.

With relatives taken care of, friends were next on the program. Bonnets were made for the new twins, a pair of socks and heavy mittens for each of Rod's brothers and sisters. Rod himself was taken for granted as part of Bill's family now, and he seemed happy and healthy in his new environment.

Helen worked with intense satisfaction on a pair of wee booties, a bonnet, and a sweater for the yet unborn baby of Nelly Shaw. She chose the daintiest pattern in her book of directions and surveyed the completed garments with intense pleasure—the fine stitch, the dainty embroidery.

There still remained the making of socks for Bill and a suit for Johnny. Helen's enthusiasm was almost exhausted. Mom Barnes and Mrs. Olson came to the rescue once again, and Smitty contrived to knit steadily until the full quota they had set for themselves had been completed.

The night of the school concert had arrived. This was an historic night in the community. Old and young, rich and poor of every race and creed presented themselves at the affair every year. Helen was surprised to find, as she helped Smitty pack the gifts and parcels that they were to take along, that she was looking forward to this special "gathering of the clans," which she had mentally termed it. It was Rod's first outing since his illness, and Smitty had written the words of the immortal "'Twas the night before Christmas" on a piece of paper for him. He was mumbling the words to himself as they travelled toward the schoolhouse in an effort to memorize every word, every pause, just as Smitty had taught him, for by arrangement with the teacher, this was to be his piece in the school program.

When they arrived at the little schoolhouse on the outskirts of the town, Bill helped Helen to alight from the caboose. The air was clear and frosty, and her breath hung in vapour before her face. She stood in the snow-filled schoolyard, while Bill tied the horses to the fence and went to get Johnny from Smitty's arms. Cars, trucks, open cutters, and sleighs of every description filled the yard around the schoolhouse. Children ran to and fro whispering excitedly, and grown-ups walked toward the building carrying bundles and boxes of every shape and size. They were greeted on every hand by "Merry Christmas," and there was an air of good-will everywhere.

As they climbed the step and opened the door, the sound of music drifted out over the night and the words of "Silent Night" came to them in mystic beauty.

The air was warm in the big room, and it was filled with the fragrance of pine needles from the tall Christmas tree that stood on the platform, lighted and heavily laden. The branches were weighted down with every conceivable trinket, and on the floor beneath it, a small mountain of ribboned and gaily wrapped parcels lay.

It has been the custom—since the days when Moosewell was only a small settlement with a few, isolated families—for families to gather each year, on the Friday before Christmas Day, to lay gifts for each other at the foot of the school Christmas tree. So tonight, the children of these early settlers, and their children's children, came from all corners of the district to the same little schoolhouse, and they laid their gifts at the foot of the tree. Only family gifts for each immediate family-circle would be kept at home for the family tree.

Helen and Smitty carried their gifts for the Hughes family, Mom Barnes, the Olsons, and Nelly Shaw and put them there amongst the rest. Suddenly, as Helen stooped with her gifts, she experienced a feeling of well-being, of belonging. These were her friends, her people—she belonged! Had she not befriended them and they her? Did this not give her a claim to their regard? For the first time, she was no longer an outsider looking in.

The program started and the children excelled. When Rod stood up and walked to the front of the platform, Helen felt a thrill of pride for him. Still pale and thinner than the other children, he stood erect in his new suit, white shirt, and coloured tie—dressed in party clothes like the other children for the first time in his life. Helen knew his mother was somewhere in the crowd and wondered what her reaction would be tonight. Then, incredibly, she heard a familiar drawl behind her: "You a stranger in these parts? Don't know that boy? Why, that's my son—my second son." There was no mistaking the pride in Hughes' voice, but a muffled sob sound came from somewhere very near him and Helen's heart went out to the mother, there, amidst the people behind her.

"'Twas the night before Christmas,
    when all through the house...."

When Rod had finished with a bow, a storm of applause shook the house, and he stepped back and sat down with the boys in his grade.

With the ending of the program, presents were distributed by a fat, jolly Santa Claus who had a laugh just exactly like Pop Barnes. Helen was so intensely interested in the way the children received and handled their gifts that she failed to hear Johnny's name called, and so it was Bill who carried his son on his shoulders up to the laughing, joking distributor of gifts. He demanded a kiss in return for a present, and Johnny stooped from his height on Bill's shoulder to give the kiss.

Then Johnny held back and rubbed Santa's chin. "It tickles," Johnny said, to everyone's delight.

There were gifts from so many neighbours that Helen was astonished, little knowing how many kind hearts amongst them went out to the young wife so far away from home. Smitty also received several gifts, for she had become known everywhere for her helpfulness. Despite the abundance of parcels that lay at her feet, Helen's mind continued to wander back to the flat, light envelope perched upon one of the branches on their tree at home. On the front was written, in Bill's handwriting, "To Helen. Not to be opened until Christmas Day." The curiosity was almost too much for her.

Most people did not open their parcels, but took them home to be added to the pile beneath their own family tree. This was not so with the small children, who ripped the fancy wrappings apart and grasped at the toys beneath. Every single child was remembered by several people. Each child had a gift from school, another from Santa Claus, and many more from neighbours, relatives, and chums. To everyone present went a bag of candy and fruit, popcorn, and cookies.

Returning to her seat after her name was called for yet another gift, Helen saw Nelly Shaw sitting inconspicuously in a corner, wrapped in an old fur coat that effected a real concealment. On her knee was a lone gift, wrapped in white tissue paper and tied with a blue ribbon. In her eyes a secret smile. Helen moved over and sat down beside her for a while and wished her a merry Christmas, asking if it would be possible for her to pay a visit soon.

"We would love to have you," Helen coaxed.

"I cannot come soon," Nelly replied. "You see, Dad and the boys have been building a little house for me over on the quarter of land Dad gave me, and my youngest brother Ed and I will be moving over there as soon as possible. Dad and Ed never did get along, but Ed is my favourite brother. Oh, I have so much to thank you for!"

"Me?" Helen spoke in surprise. Then Helen went on, "I will come to see you as soon as you are settled." Nelly answered that she would be looking forward to the visit.

The new, young preacher stood up just then to give them all a Christmas message of hope and encouragement, and soon the party broke up. Then the saddle horses, teams, sleighs, and cars steamed along the highway. The little schoolhouse was locked and left alone, silent until the bell should ring again and the holidays be over.

Helen had, in one way, been dreading the arrival of the yuletide season. That was one of the reasons she threw herself into such an ecstasy of work and activity. But now that it had arrived, she found that in some inexplicable way, it seemed to supply the link she needed between the old life and the new. She thought of home and friends with less heartbreak, and she became determined to make a place for herself amongst the new with an enthusiasm she had thought impossible.

When Christmas morning came, Johnny was the centre of attention and he knew it, acting up and being spoiled by everyone in the house. Rod, too, was flushed with happiness, not the least of which was caused by the fact that he had seen Bill ride off that morning with a box of Christmas food for his family.

Smitty had made only one request, and that was that her friend, Mr. Patrick, be invited to spend the day with them, explaining that his family lived some many miles away in another province. Knowing that that sort of thing was typical of Smitty, neither Bill nor Helen were surprised, and they welcomed the idea gladly. "A new face in the old house will help relieve the monotony," Helen thought. They waited some time for Mr. Patrick, but when he failed to arrive, they began to open their gifts that lay under the tree that Bill had cut down and brought home.

Johnny's presents were opened and admired first. Then came Rod's, which were few and useful. Bill suggested that as Helen had the most important gift of all, she should wait until the last, and so she waited until Bill and Smitty had opened their parcels and duly admired the contents, but she could scarcely contain her curiosity.

At last her turn came, and she held up the envelope and asked Bill, "May I open this now?"

"Yes, Darling, you may." There was something so serious and so sad in his tone that she hesitated. "Go on, open it," he went on.

Then, with all eyes upon her, she tore the flap. As the contents fell out onto her lap she held her breath, and then tears filled her eyes and voice, and they ran down her cheeks. "Why, Bill! Two adult's tickets to England!"

"Just like a woman to cry when she gets something she wants," said Bill.

Smitty took Johnny by the hand and looked in a meaningful way at Rod, who understood and followed her to the kitchen, leaving Bill and Helen alone.

"But Bill—there are two tickets. Would you go too?"

"I will take you back, Helen," he sang, but there was heartbreak in his dark eyes as she probed them deep.

"But, Bill, you don't really want to go. Wouldn't you rather stay here?"

"Do you think I could live without you, Sweetheart?" he asked, and pulled her into his arms.

"But how can you leave this place—your farm, the friends you have known since you were born?"

"I love them, Helen," said with a catch in his throat, "but I love you more. And you cannot seem to find happiness here, so I will take you back to where you want to be."

"Bill, Bill. I want to be here! I love it too—this farm, these people. They need me and—Bill—I need them, too! I don't want to go anywhere else, and I will never be afraid again, now that I know... that I know... you love me."

No words could express the joy in Bill's heart as he listened to this outburst from his wife—the young wife he loved with his whole being. They stood apart when a knock came to the door, jumping up from the one chair that had held them both. Helen started toward the door to open it, patting her hair straight as she walked. The young minister stood at the door and Helen looked at him in surprise.

"Why... come in!" and when she spoke there was happiness in the inflection of her voice.

"I... I am sorry that I am late," he apologized. "You see, the Christmas present I ordered for Smitty just arrived. The post office was not open, but Mrs. Barnes knew I was waiting for the parcel and she let me have it."

"Well, if you want to see Smitty, go on into the kitchen. Whatever she is making in there smells mighty good to me. We'll eat about three o'clock if the turkey is cooked, so don't take up too much of Smitty's attention."

But the young man had already disappeared and the kitchen door was swinging closed behind him. In a few minutes, Rod led Johnny back into the living room and asked, "Is it safe to come in here now? I'm having an awful time—just when the eats were almost ready, too. Hope she don't forget and let things burn or something."

"What are you talking about?" asked Helen.

"You'll see," he replied sagely.

It was a long time before Smitty and Alexander Patrick came back to the living room, and Smitty did not come to announce dinner—much to Rod's disappointment. Instead, she walked toward Bill and Helen and held out her left hand. On the third finger sparkled a lovely diamond. She looked at Mr. Patrick proudly as she said, "I wanted to tell you before, but Alex insisted on everything being done decently and in order, so we waited for the ring to arrive—and it nearly didn't!" As for Alexander Patrick, dinner was the least of his worries just then. He was still in a glorious daze.

"It's going to be rather nice having a preacher in the family," was Bill's laughing comment. And so, Christmas Day came and went, but at times, as the day wore on, it seemed to Helen that her happiness was more than she could bear.

Chapter Nineteen

With Christmas over, time was drawing toward the new year, and soon after that came the day when Bill said, "Did you hear the latest? Hughes is suing me! Charging me with contributing to the delinquency of a juvenile. Says I'm alienating Rod from his home and parents." And he laughed heartily.

But Helen was worried. Could the man make the charge stick? It was true that Bill had encouraged the boy to stay, had bought him clothing and promised him an education. What attitude would the mother take? Helen knew that Rod's mother had been very dependent on her young son, and that both parents must sorely miss the hard-working, intelligent boy around the place.

"What do you think, Rod?" Bill asked the boy. "Do you want to go back?"

With wisdom beyond his years, the boy had studied the problem from many angles. "Well, it's like this," he answered. "I could never like Dad after what he done to me. It ain't the beatin' that I mind so much as his sellin' my horse, though I knew he'd a done it sooner or later. And I want t'help Mother, but I believe I can help her more by goin' t'school and gettin' a good job. Then I can buy her the things she needs—a washin' machine, clothes, things like that. I know Dad won't ever get'm for her, and even if I stay here and work for wages, he'll take them from me t'buy liquor. I can help here, on the farm, and continue to go to school, and—if you still want me—I'd be happy to stay."

"Well, Son, you tell all that to the judge. We'll see. Now that Smitty is going to leave us, we will not only want you, we shall need you."

When the case came up in court and the trial was on, the courtroom was crowded. Bill's name was called, and he was probably the most confident defendant who ever faced the magistrate. He told of the events of the night of the storm in plain, simple language.

"I would not have turned a dog away that night," was all he said in his own defence.

Then Doc Carney was called as a defence witness and corroborated the story, giving as his opinion that the boy would have died but for the care and nursing that the McElroys had given him so lovingly.

The man who bought the horse had been subpoenaed to appear in court, and he told of the deal he had made with Hughes. He also mentioned the sum of money he had given Hughes for the horse, an amount grossly under the value of the animal.

Smitty was next on the stand and gave her account of the events of that night. Others followed and, last of all, Rod himself was called.

In summing up, the magistrate said, "The case is, of course, dismissed for lack of evidence to substantiate the charges, but in this trial several things have come to light of which I take a very serious view. Here is a horse, bought and sold without a legal bill of sale passing hands. A child is beaten and tossed into a storm in below-zero weather, yet no alarm is raised by other members of the family. A family, by the way, continually undernourished and living in a state of neglect, yet none of the community intervened to report the case to the authorities. The only friend that the children in the family seem to have is rewarded by a charge being laid against him by one of the parents.

"I suggest that you, Mr. McElroy, apply through the proper channels for legal guardianship of this boy. In the meantime, he will become a charge of the province and will be placed in your care. I, myself, will have the case for the rest of the family thoroughly investigated."

On the way home from the trial, the McElroy family stopped off at the post office and general store, where Mom Barnes handed Helen a tiny envelope along with the other mail.

"How's your son, John?" asked Helen as she took the mail and then said, "Thank you."

"Oh, he's fine. He's off to see his new girlfriend today," she said with a grin.

Helen pulled a small card from the envelope. On it was a picture of a baby's shoe, and below was written, "Just arrived." Inside, the script ran:

Born to Nelly Shaw,
a boy, James Edward
Weight: 7.5 lbs.
When: 8th January 1947

Chapter Twenty

Pain wakened Helen. She lay in the darkness and listened to Bill's quiet breathing beside her. Johnny turned over in his bed and laughed aloud in his sleep. The house was quiet save for that, until a log in the big heater crackled and the fire began to roar again.

She lay there, trying to grasp onto courage with both hands, until the pain roiled up and swamped her again. She caught her breath in a short, dry sob as pain enveloped her again and again, leaving her, when it ebbed, exhausted and beaten.

This was the day she had dreaded and feared through all the long winter months that lay behind. Why had she allowed herself to be lulled into a sense of false security?

As she lay there in the ebb and flow of the pain that beset her, the darkness around her seemed sinister, mocking. "Where," it taunted her with its very voicelessness, "is the fool's paradise you have lived in for the past few weeks? How," it queried, "can your deep love for Bill help you now?"

She was miles away from the nearest neighbour, at an almost unbelievable distance from doctor or hospital—fear above, below, on every side of her. What could she do now? Had she not been a fool from first to last? Home, Dad, Sue— all had been within her grasp, but she had chosen to ignore her difficulty till now it was upon her, suddenly, without warning, in the dark hours of the morning!

She felt the pain recede and advance upon her again—hot, searing, merciless. She must have screamed, for suddenly there was Bill, bending over her anxiously. There was a light.

Once again the world seemed secure. Of course she had been right after all! Bill was here. He would take care of her. He would help her fight this battle against pain—a pain so overwhelming. He had taken her in his arms now, and words of endearment, of courage and concern, flowed from his lips. He was a bulwark for her poor, shivering heart; a bulwark against the darkness, the distance, and the cold. He knew what to do, and he would do it.

Smitty had already come and disappeared, and Helen heard her moving quietly through the house. Bill laid her gently back on the pillow, and she rested till he came back and lifted her in his arms, wrapped her tight in a warm woollen blanket, and carried her out to the caboose. A fire was burning in the little heater; a lantern swung from the roof; a bedroll lay on the floor, ready to receive her aching body.

Helen looked around her as they emerged from the house. The darkness had gone, bright stars scintillated down upon the snow, causing it to glisten as though bejewelled. It was al- most as clear as day, although it was bitterly cold, as if the winter was making one last attempt to assert its authority before admitting defeat and giving way to spring.

The horses were prancing, their breath floating away in feathery wreaths. They were anxious to be off. The four miles to Moosewell slid past in a delirium of pain and torment, but fear no longer haunted her.

Upon reaching the Barnes' general store, she was quickly transferred to a swift car. Mom Barnes took Smitty's place beside Helen while Bill drove on in the night. Smitty returned home with the team to Rod and Johnny, who lay asleep in the old log house, unaware of the drama that had moved about them.

Helen fought for her breath and held hard onto her courage every mile of that swift trip along the road to Cross Town and the hospital. They arrived at the big arched gateway just as dawn was rising up over the edge of the distant hills in a rosy glow.

When they rang the night bell, a black-garbed Sister of Mercy—her face framed in a stiffly-starched white halo—opened the door for them. Soon Helen was taken from Bill's arms and carried away beyond his sight.

Mom Barnes drove off home after giving Bill definite instructions to phone. He was left standing there, ill at ease, until the big front door swung open again and Doc Carney came through in answer to an urgent telephone call. Throwing a nod and an encouraging grin in Bill's direction, he climbed the stairs, two at a time, and then he too disappeared.

The Sister who had opened the door came back and invited Bill into the office. "I must get your name and all the details," she told him with a decidedly French accent.

"McElroy," he told her. "William G. McElroy."

She lifted her head in a startled way. "But... Would you be Bill McElroy?" she asked.

"Yes," he assured her.

"Then we will stop for nothing. We will go to your friend. He has been calling and calling for you in his delirium, and so I planned to tell the doctor, but the doctor has been too busy. Three babies he has delivered since yesterday noon, when this man arrived."

With something very like astonishment, Bill followed her along the corridor and turned into a small ward where there were four narrow, white beds. Around one of them tall, white screens were placed, and it was to this one that the Sister led him. There lay a pitiful figure, old and emaciated, with black eyes sparkling bright with the heat of his fever. There lay—very evidently near the end of his long journey—Jimmy Blackcrow, the friend and companion of the Bill McElroy who now lay in the cemetery on One Mile Corner.

"How did he get here?" Bill demanded.

"He arrived but yesterday. The pilot who took him to his trapline two years ago has been dropping supplies regularly ever since. This last trip, as he dropped supplies on the edge of the lakeshore where this trapper lived, he noticed there was no smoke coming from the cabin. On his way back, he set his plane down on the ice and proceeded to investigate. There he found the old man lying ill on his bunk—almost frozen, almost gone. He has been delirious since last night, but he was quite rational when he came, and he called for you and the good Father. The Father came and the patient asked him to write. I myself was one of the witnesses. He bequeathed to you all of his fur catch and a box of money that he brought with him in the plane, and gave it into the Father's keeping."

Bill was deeply touched and thought very little of the furs or the box of money, thinking that at most it would amount to two- or three-hundred dollars. Unable to go to Helen as he ached to do, he sat at the bedside of his old friend and heard his own name repeated with a pathetic urgency. Jimmy Blackcrow lay dark and shrunken beneath the white sheets, the long black braids on each side of his head were laid out on the pillow. Never again would he look upon this world, nor would he know that his call for his friend had been answered.

So it was that on the day that Jimmy Blackcrow died, baby Sue was born. Helen lay back weakly, and looked up at Bill with a proud look in her eyes.

"Darling," she said, "I will never doubt again. The North is a wonderful place. I know now, for a certainty."

"Are you quite sure?"

"Yes, Darling. I am quite sure."

"Well then, I will tell you the end of a story I began one night, long ago." And he told her of the death of Jimmy Blackcrow. They were quietly thinking their own thoughts for a while after Bill had finished speaking, and then Helen spoke. "Now we must begin to think of Smitty's wedding!"

"Yes. Just as soon as you are well enough."

Points of Discussion:

1. Approximately 48,000 war brides entered Canada through Pier 21 in Halifax, Nova Scotia, following World War II. What is the significance of this event? In what ways can factual and fictional accounts of the war bride experience recognize that significance?

2. Bill struggles with battle fatigue and the loss of his property after returning to Canada from World War II. How are Bill's experiences similar or different to war veterans returning to Canada from post–World War II missions?

3. In her writing, Eileen MacDonald uses language typical of the post-war era. What are some examples of this?

4. In what ways can Helen's immigrant experience be compared to the experiences of women immigrating to Canada today?

5. While homesteading on the prairies, Helen experiences both isolation and community. How does Helen rely on the vision of a homeland to help her meet the challenges of integrating into a new society?

6. In the novel, which events help Helen feel a sense belonging? Does Helen come to identify herself as a Canadian?

7. There are several promises and voids in this story. What conflicts are set up as a result of the main characters believing in something, but finding that their expectations are unmet? How are these conflicts resolved?

Acknowledgements

I, Rebekah Allen (the project manager and granddaughter of the author, Eileen MacDonald), extend a heartfelt and resounding thank you to several people for their tangible support in this novel's fruition. From immediate and extended family, friends, and neighbours, I've received moral support as well as feedback for the continuation of the project. The following people deserve special recognition for their significant hours of support (ranging from typing out the original document to proofreading):

Alice Brown, Pullman, Washington
Maggie Melley, Airdrie, Alberta
Jane Leslie, Calgary, Alberta
Sheila McIlwain, Lacombe, Alberta
Nancy Dempster, Airdrie, Alberta
Will, Sam and Jon Allen, you are my heroes!

Lastly, without Jennifer Kaddoura, this publication would not have been completed. Her professionalism and editing expertise ensured the project's continuity and brought the novel to life through a comprehensive review of the manuscript, all the while steadfastly respecting and preserving Eileen's voice.

Publisher's Note

The diction in this narrative remains true to the period of writing. Editorial choices in this posthumous publication were made with intentions to maintain the author's style and voice as well as to make the manuscript accessible for a modern audience. Linguistic and social sensitivities are ever-evolving, so modern resources were consulted to update terminology in today's context. For guidance, the *Oxford Canadian Dictionary (2nd ed.)*, *The Chicago Manual of Style (16th ed.)* and *The Canadian Press Stylebook (17th ed.)* were consulted.

Specifically, use of the term Indian was carefully considered. Consulted resources indicate that, at the time of this novel's publication, usage of this term is in a shifting state. While some consider it outdated, there are members of Canada's Aboriginal community who maintain a preference for use of the term. The consulted resources indicated that the term may be most appropriate in historical works. In consideration of the author's voice, the original term was maintained as a reflection of the period in which the narrative was written. This and all other editorial choices are not intended to offend or exclude alternative perspectives; they are considered opportunities to invite discussions on the evolution of language and acceptable terminology.

For more information, or to buy more copies of this book, go to PromiseInTheVoid.com

Or contact PageMaster:
orders@pagemaster.ca
780-425-9303
PageMasterPublishing.ca/Shop